WINNIE'S TONGUE

Also by Nic Labriola

Francis and the Animals
Naming the Mannequins

Winnie's Tongue

A Novel

Nic Labriola

INSOMNIAC PRESS

Copyright © 2015 by Nic Labriola

All rights reserved. No part of this publication may be reproduced, stored in a retrieval system or transmitted, in any form or by any means, without the prior written permission of the publisher or, in the case of photocopying or other reprographic copying, a licence from Access Copyright, 1 Yonge Street, Suite 1900, Toronto, ON M5E 1E5

Library and Archives Canada Cataloguing in Publication

Labriola, Nic, 1981-, author
Winnie's tongue / Nic Labriola.

Issued in print and electronic formats.
ISBN 978-1-55483-148-7 (pbk.).--ISBN 978-1-55483-160-9 (html)

I. Title.

PS8623.A333W55 2015   C813'.6   C2015-902471-4
                                      C2015-902472-2

The publisher gratefully acknowledges the support of the Canada Council, the Ontario Arts Council, and the Department of Canadian Heritage through the Canada Book Fund.

Printed and bound in Canada

Insomniac Press
520 Princess Avenue, London, Ontario, Canada, N6B 2B8
www.insomniacpress.com

For Samantha

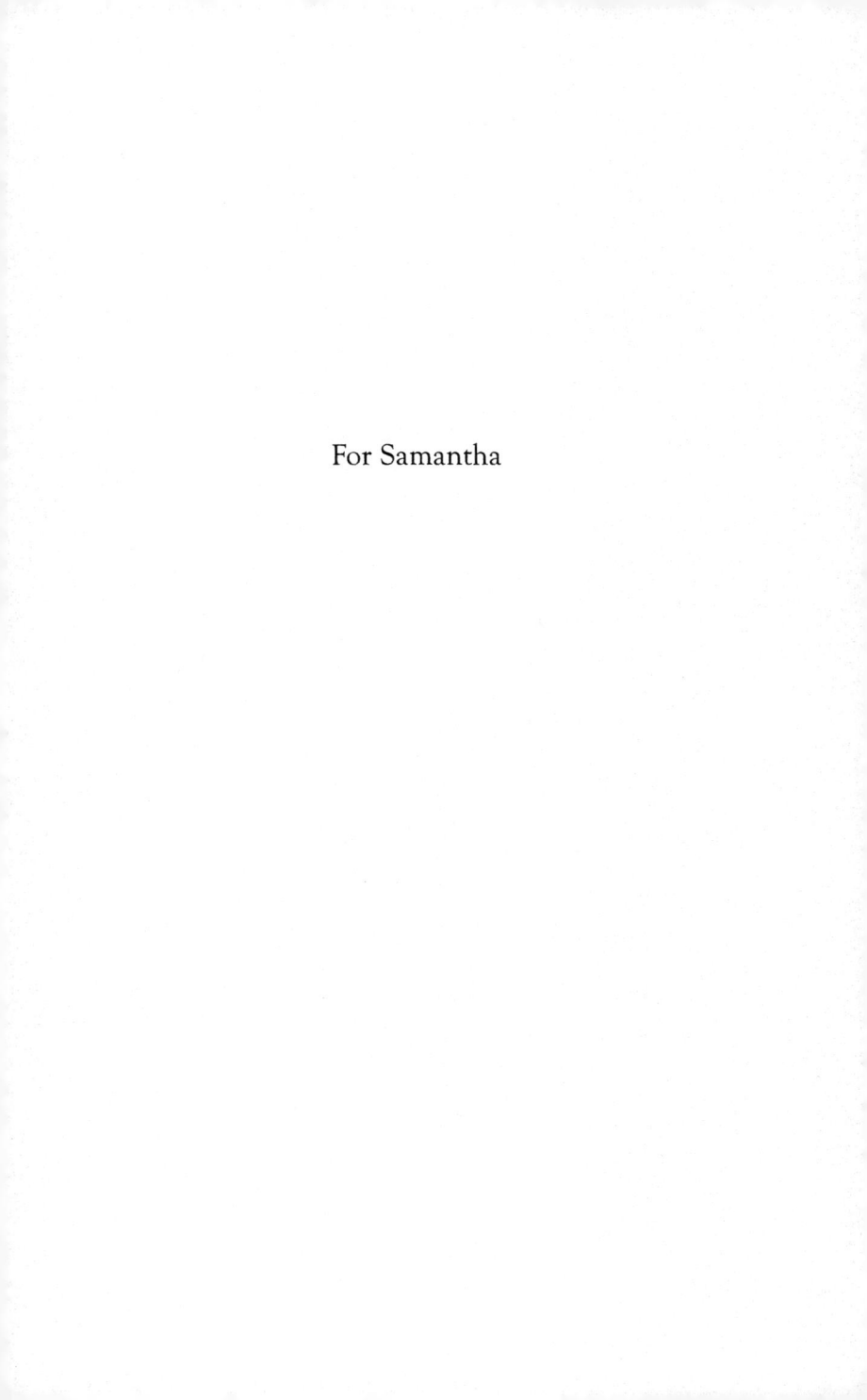

Acknowledgements

Chapters One and Two of *Winnie's Tongue* previously appeared as the short story "Tongue" in the collection *Francis and the Animals* (Leaping Lion, 2012).

Thanks, as always, for the love and enthusiasm of my family: my parents, Tony and Jo, and my pals, Anthony, Michelle, Christina, and Joanna.

Thanks to Samantha for helping me shape the novel.

Thanks to Mike O'Connor and Insomniac Press.

Thanks to Dan Varrette for his fine editorial work.

Thanks to the Ontario Arts Council, an agency of the Government of Ontario, for supporting the completion of *Winnie's Tongue* through a Writers' Works in Progress Grant.

1

Caught again and doing my best to end things with some nameless bastard with whom I shared a bed. Packing up my clothes into grocery bags, I made it to the front door before he found me wriggling and held onto my long, Raggedy Ann-red hair and forced his fingers inside my mouth. Strangers passed us on the street, unnerved, accustomed to domestic disputes, freak shows, and hunting in the south end. He almost had me back inside, and I'd already lost my high-heeled, black leather boots, kicking, when Constantine arrived. I sized him at well over six feet, 250 pounds plus. His long, golden-blond locks made him look more like an overgrown kid than a man maybe in his late twenties. But what struck me most and left me staring was his enormous, wet tongue. The thing barely fit inside his mouth. Red blubber emerged from his pharynx and hanging ball in croaking accordion folds that forced him into operatic reptile talk. Indecipherable.

"Lead ear go! Lead ear go! Lead ear go!"

Drooling like a bulldog sucking on a lemon, the

tongue popped out and drooped all the way down the chin, quivering like a wet fish, whipping around and smacking against the nose. My boyfriend's rage melted into a puddle by his feet at the sight of it—disturbed, staring, mesmerized. Constantine flexed his wondrous thing and stuck it straight out in front of him like a demon child on a playground. His face was as red as a beet, and his nostrils flared. Nervous laughter from my boyfriend masked his fear until he coughed a little, whimpered, and went silent. Then he let me go.

But with no place really to go, being on the run since sixteen, and that final wrestling match with my father that had broken his arm, I followed Constantine's tongue to a tiny room he rented above an ice cream parlour not far from where I'd been staying. Of course, I wouldn't learn that his name was Constantine until later. I took to calling the man Tongue. I followed Tongue through a narrow, slanted, brown-carpeted walkup, three flights, through a haze of vanilla and burning coconut. He carried my clothes, heavy with each clumping step. Then, turning at the door before entering, in something like Spanish, I think I heard him say, "Mi *casa es su casa.*" But I could never be sure. He needed a translator: His *b*'s were *p*'s, his *f*'s were *v*'s, his *o*'s were *ah*'s, and his *th*'s didn't exist. I swear to God he was all over the place. I did my best to sort through his fractured phonetics. He had two kind, bulging eyes, packed inside his head, that looked like healing stones used to cure the sick.

Inside, the place was decorated with function and luck. Found furniture: a reused table, a patched-up couch, and a mismatched mattress and box spring, one king, one queen. A big metal fan was buzzing in the corner of the living room. Clothes were strewn from one end of the place to the other. There was a whiff of rot coming off the blackened bananas on the kitchen counter, swarming with fruit flies next to about eight or nine different kinds of breakfast cereal boxes. The door closed with the weight of my sudden vulnerability. This is how I always enter a man's house. And with the allure of the tongue's rescue fading, I locked myself in the bathroom, without saying a word, and stared at the giant rubber duckies on his shower curtain.

I started to search through his medicine cabinet for evidence of serial killings, disorders, kinks, or other addictions. I looked for something to explain his extraordinary mouth, but the toothbrush was a normal size, and he used ordinary mouthwash. No strange bits of headgear or elastic devices to accompany such a mutation. I looked for a wooden spoon that he might sleep with to prevent him from swallowing the bloody thing, but there was nothing.

I pried open a window above the toilet, looked out onto a fire escape. I had slipped through windows before. I climbed onto a radiator, shimmied out, and landed safely on steps lined with wrought iron. Escape was simple for me. I felt as if I'd been born that way and had freed myself at birth from my mother's body and never looked back.

But when I finally made it to street level, I did look back. I saw Tongue going into the ice cream parlour, aptly named Creamed Dreams. There was a neon sign in the window that at one time must have read "You scream, I scream, we all scream for ice cream," but most of the lettering was burned out, so all that kept flashing now was "we all scream, we all scream, we all scream" over and over again. He was shapeless, grey. A rock that entered the gaudy shop with its shoddy, peeling purple, orange, and red paint job.

I crossed the road to avoid being seen and took cover in the doorway of a cash loans store next to a rank twenty-four-hour laundromat. I watched him study a menu behind a counter, banter with a man wearing a paper hat, sample something pink from a tiny wooden spoon. His tongue was more moist and radiant than the desserts. He bought two waffle cones with cherries on top and left.

Back out on the street, he held the cones in his meat hooks as the tip of his tongue worked away at one. It was like watching a camel going at a slab of salt. Seeing him that way, a cartoon animal, or even just an animal, dispelled my fears.

"Hey!" I yelled to him.

"Heee!" he yelled back, not surprised to see me. "'Tss cherry!" And he held out a cone for me.

We ate the cherry ice cream cones on the roof of his building. Although it was only a few stories up, I was high enough to see all that I wanted of the city. High enough for someone to commit suicide and still be able to glimpse the world before landing. We leaned against some wooden fencing.

"Makes you want to jump," I told him, but he didn't agree.

"Naw it don't."

"Feels like a giant hand could reach up over the edge, grab me, and pull me over. And I'd let it pull me over and down, all the way down, as long as I could watch the crash."

"Naw it don't," he said again.

"It's like staring at a rushing waterfall. Or like the second before a train comes by.... Makes you want to jump."

But for him, it didn't. He acted like he hadn't heard me and continued to lick away like a lizard.

"Ever drop acid?" I asked.

He stopped his licking, cocked his head to one side, and looked at me, thinking about it.

"You put it under your tongue and just let it sit there until it dissolves. It makes you see visions."

"Oh, dreams?" he asked.

"Almost."

Tongue came towards me and stood inches away. Tilting his medicine ball head back, he closed his eyes and opened his mouth. His tongue was a bright flamingo pink now from the ice cream. I placed a strip inside and took a hit myself. Tongue winced. He clamped his mouth shut. I heard the molars in his head snap like a trap closing.

"Do I choo?" he asked through his clenched teeth. "No taste."

I saw his jaw muscles bulge. Told him to let it melt. He lay sprawled on the tarred roof like a tranquilized horse waiting to be put down. His breathing was slow and deep. I was falling under and felt as if he were sucking in all the air around us. He turned to look at me and whispered something that sounded like, "Melting."

My trip took a wrong turn when I heard him howl. Tongue was rigid on his back now, a cruciform staring up at the sky. His piercing cry was neither pleasure nor pain. I tried shushing him, lulling him back under, because the brute was ruining it for me.

"Melting!" he screamed.

He sprung into action. Took shape out of his shadow on the rooftop. Climbed up over the railing. I went after him, but he had already managed to climb over to the other side. I grabbed him by the back of his belt and braced my feet against the fencing. Tongue continued to screech, and he arched his body down towards the street. I wasn't going to be responsible for this idiot's death, although in that instant I was convinced his entire body was made of rubber and that, if he did plummet, he'd surely just bounce back up like some huge, red utility ball.

"Flying!" he continued with outstretched arms. "Lead me go!"

His belt was cutting into my fingers. A small line of blood began to form. I was losing circulation in my arm. With my free hand, I grabbed him by his thick, curly, blond hair and pulled his head back towards the safety of the ledge. Tongue began to laugh even though I was ripping out his goddamn locks from the roots. His disgusting tongue protruded in spasm from the vibrations of his belly. I reached for it, seized the slimy thing in my right hand, and started to pull. It writhed and flicked in my grip. I dug my nails into the frenulum and dragged it toward me. His massive body followed. He slunk back on top of the roof, mumbling, coughing, and chanting, "Humpity Dumpity sat on a wall. Huppity Duppity had a great fall."

2

We must have fallen asleep soon after and spent most of the night up there, but I don't remember how I ended up in his bed the next morning, or if he had spent the night beside me. When I awoke, I was alone, and I found myself staring up at a wrestling poster on the ceiling. The man in the picture wore green and yellow face paint. He was baring his bottom teeth as if they were fangs. His greasy hair was long and swept back. There were ribbons tied to the bends in his rippling and glistening orange arms and legs. Getting up, I smacked my knee into the bedside table and upset a large stash of assorted candies stored in a big red pail by the clock radio. The collision sent gumdrops and countless other candies scattering onto the floor, jumping and rolling around. I bent down and grabbed a stick of red licorice, and I started gnawing on it to take away the taste of my morning breath.

I heard Tongue singing opera in the other room. The previous day's exertion had taken its toll on my body, and I could barely get out of the enormous bed. Tongue was puttering away in the kitchen. I found him hulking over a hot plate, scrambling eggs. A small black and white television played morning cartoons through poor reception.

"Scrambies," he said when he saw me.

I went inside the bathroom and saw a shipwreck in the mirror. The details of how I'd washed up with this gargantuan chef were unclear. I was in no shape to go to a funeral. I searched my pockets for my father's death notice:

Surrounded by his family, Benny McKeagan passed away peacefully at St. Michael's Hospital on Tuesday. Services will be held Friday at 1 p.m. at Eternal Hope.

Dearest Daddy's death had not surprised me when I came across it at the back of the newspaper. It was the idea that he had been surrounded by his family that was tough to take. I hadn't seen or spoken to anyone from my clan in eight years, and I didn't want to believe that any of them had given him any comfort or forgiveness when he expired.

I tied my hair back tight into a ponytail and joined Tongue for breakfast. He had arranged the eggs into a face on my plate. Burned bacon strips in the shape of a mouth smiled up at me. A blueberry muffin nose.

"Any coffee?" I asked.

"Yuck," said Tongue.

He wore a tight, yellowed wife-beater and baggy, brown cotton pants. He stared at his television show as he lapped happily at his meal.

"Want to go to a funeral?" I asked him.

"When?"

"This afternoon."

"Don't dig egg?" he asked through a mouthful of meat.

"Yuck," I said.

Tongue and I went to a Salvation Army store a few blocks away from his house. Neither of us had anything appropriate to wear to the cemetery, although I didn't know exactly what would be appropriate to wear to the burial of a madman. I knew it wasn't black. The store smelled like mildew; it was a familiar odour. Racks of used clothes sprawled out before us. They reminded me of all the people who must be alive out there, sweating out armpits, outgrowing dresses, ripping the seats of pants, spilling fluids, making stains. A mess.

Tongue wandered off into the back of the place while I started sorting through some of the rotted ruins. I knew my old man would spin in his stinking grave if I showed up to his funeral in a pair of cut-off jeans and a halter top. But if I were to wear something like that, I would only be choosing it because of him—to disgrace him. And if I were to wear something less shocking, if I were to wear black, I'd still only be choosing it because of him. So I was trapped.

Tongue appeared out of nowhere wearing a pair of leather chaps. They didn't fit. He bulged out of them like swollen fruit.

"Cute," I said.

He was pleased and galloped off.

With every item I picked up—every blouse, skirt, jacket, and pantsuit—I couldn't picture myself wearing it without seeing my father's dead eyes leering at me. Devouring me. There was nothing I could put on that he did not have control over. I could never dress myself without first reflecting on how I would appear to him, even now that he was a corpse. So I decided I'd wear what I had on.

Tongue emerged from the change room in a massive, white suit. He was beautiful. The intense ivory draped his powerful body in a way that I did not think was possible because he was so large. I couldn't imagine another man owning and wearing that same suit before Tongue.

"Constantine in gabardine," Tongue said proudly.

Tongue donated his brown pants to the store and paid for his suit, and we left. I was walking beside a white wall now. A brilliant sun reflected off his towering square shoulders and massive back. It was hard to look at him without squinting. Passing a garden on the way to the cemetery, Tongue found some flowers.

"No way," I said. "No goddamn flowers."

"Not for him," he said.

Tongue ripped out a couple of pink begonias and inserted a stem into the buttonhole of his new jacket. The flower opened up on his lapel, the petals made all the more vivid by the whiteness that surrounded them.

"Well, ain't you perdy?" I said.

"You're perdy," he said, and he gave me the other flower to put somewhere on my body. I stuck the thing behind my ear, knowing full well that the pink would clash with my red hair and lipstick.

By the time we arrived, the service was already underway. Tongue and I took cover behind a slate mausoleum. We sat on its steps. From a distance, I saw a swarm of blue and black bugs around a hole in the earth. Fifteen men huddled together around a shiny box. I knew it must be my family because of the brassy, ginger hair. My cheeks burned thinking about all that wiry, orange fur. I began to gag as if I were swallowing talcum powder. Tongue peeked around the corner and started to laugh. I looked back at them. My brothers and uncles were taking turns pouring whiskey on my father's grave, weeping. I wanted to rip the priest's eyes out.

Tongue went ahead of me and joined the circle of male mourners. He towered over the others. They all looked like headstones to me. Tongue waited patiently for his turn to pour. When it came, he clutched the bottle with both hands and began to sprinkle the whiskey over the casket. My brothers soon realized that Tongue was misplaced when he wouldn't stop pouring. He was now walking in circles around the grave, lost inside his own ritual.

"That's enough, son," the priest said.

But Tongue continued to pour.

"I said that's enough."

My brothers and uncles intervened and tried to grab the bottle away from Tongue. He dodged them, holding onto the bottle, and weaved his way through them until they managed to encircle him entirely. Tongue held the bottle high above their heads. I could no longer see him except for his long arm that emerged high above the group. I could hear him calling to me. I ran over.

Tongue was fighting them off, desperate to keep the bottle from spilling. He managed to knock a few of the men over. The pack opened up, all of them panting, exchanging their tears for rage. That's when they saw me. I wondered if I looked as transformed and ravaged to them as they did to me. The years in between had not been kind to my brothers, and I had to pull back double chins, remove beer bellies, strip away beards and moustaches to find the faces of my past. They must have been rearranging pieces of me to match the memory because a sudden stillness among them took over when I got close enough for them to recognize their long-lost sister.

Tongue's begonia had been ripped into pieces, and his face was seething red, but that white suit was still impeccably white. He freed himself from the remaining hands that held onto him and walked over to me. He handed me the bottle of whiskey, put his arm around my shoulders, and led me to the grave.

I emptied the entire bottle of booze over my father's box. The men just stood there, staring, watching me do it. Then, clutching the neck of the bottle, I smashed it against the headstone. Glass shattered and spit into the air. Tongue sprung back from the explosion, as did the boys. I looked down at my hand. Blood mixed with whiskey in my palm. I brought it to my mouth and licked at the small wound with my tongue. Then I spit on my father's grave.

3

The makeshift bandage, Tongue's tie wrapped tight around my mangled hand, managed to soak up most of the blood. But in the tussle that followed, red stained his white suit like burn marks. I was smeared across the entire scene, glistening on the coffin, my war paint blotting my bloated brothers' wrists and cheeks. Tongue had to lift me up, hoisted me high on his massive shoulder. I fit inside the fold of his arm, which encircled my small waist. He was galloping away from the gravesite, and I was bouncing in the air, weightless, my hair whipping with the rhythm of his lumbering body.

We escaped the werewolves then. Tongue was wild, panting, and I started to laugh.

"Hallelujah! Hallelujah!" His breathing was thick. Spittle hit me in the face. I could see that his tongue was forced from his mouth as he tried to regain control. He was wide-eyed and wheezing. The fit silenced my cackling.

"Put me down."

"Hallelujah! Hallelujah!"

"Yeah, Hallelujah. Put me down."

We lay flat on our backs in the grass behind a patch of trees in the old section of the cemetery, where eroded headstones had crumbled down to stumps—a pile of rock. I lay on a grave that I saw marked "Winifred." Tongue's stone read "Billy."

"I'm Winnie from now on," I told him. "You can be Billy."

"Who?"

"Billy." I pointed to the name etched in brittle stone. "Must have died some time ago."

"Hallelujah," he said again.

The broken-down tombstones comforted me. I was glad to be renamed, and I felt a kind of energy coming up from Winnie's rubble.

"I'm Winnie now, okay? Call me Winnie."

And I pictured the woman who lay beneath me. No doubt she'd turned to dirt long ago. Pushing through the box that contained what remained were the strangling, reaching roots of the oak that stood nearby, shading me and my 250-pound puffing angel. I reached for a roxy inside a copper pillbox I had in my pocket. Bit the pill and chewed on the bitter machinery powder until the electric shock seized my jaw and spit formed at the corners of my mouth. It was a welcomed calm, though my heart was still racing, and I felt my hips detach as wind sprinkled chalk dust on my spine.

"I hated his fat guts."

"Yeah?"

"I'm glad he's dead."

"Yeah?"

"I want a haircut. When we get back home, will you cut my hair?" I pulled at the mess on my head.

Tongue didn't respond, but his panting finally stopped, suddenly, like a thirsty dog investigating a sound. He cocked his head to one side and began searching for something inside his pants. Pulled out a pocket knife and handed it to me, smiling. It was a marvel in Swiss engineering. It wasn't just some keychain. It had to be four inches long. It felt good in my hand. The blade opened, sharp enough to slit a pig's throat, or any throat. It also had a saw blade, a pair of tweezers, a toothpick, a screwdriver, a fork and spoon, and, yes, a tiny, perfect pair of scissors. Tongue regarded the thing with wonder, proud of his tool. I was happy to see it too.

"I want you to cut my hair."

"You first!"

And he sat up against the tombstone barber chair. His back straight and arms stiff at his sides. His hair was a mass of curls that seemed impenetrable. Knotted, wet with sweat. I'd need garden shears to tame that bush. But running my fingers through as I sat on the edge of Winnie's rock, I found it soft, undamaged. It was deep, and my fingers reached a boiling scalp. I didn't want to cut it. I felt as though I'd be disrupting the flow of something sacred.

"I don't want to cut it."

"Make it like a lion's," he roared.

But I didn't know what that meant, so I just cut one lock and let it fall in his lap. Tongue began to blow hard and spit as if there were a beard in his mouth, as if I'd shaved him clean to his bull head. Instead of cutting any further, I pulled his mane back into a ponytail, although there was barely enough to make a bunch, and secured it with an elastic band. I patted him on his head. Wished I had a sucker to give him.

"There you go, Billy."

"Now you," he said, jumping to his feet and snatching the knife from me. He was too eager, and I was starting to get off my demented rebirth idea. I grabbed at my chemically fixed hair. It felt like charred straw. Just the front part, I thought.

"If I'm gonna be Winnie, I need bangs."

"Right."

"A fringe. The front part, here." I pulled my crimson hair tight down in front of my chest. "Cut here," I instructed.

Tongue reached out and clutched my hand that held my hair for support. He was serious now and abandoned his excitement for intense focus. He stuck his huge tongue out and fixed it between his teeth. I knew he meant business.

"Cut here!" I repeated. As he delayed, I was losing my nerve more and more, and so I closed my eyes, hoping he'd just start hacking. I heard him take a deep elephant breath like he was about to dive into a swamp.

"Cut here!" I was screaming now.

The slice flashed across my face. Tongue held my hair out in front of him like a child hunter's first catch—a red squirrel by the tail, limp in his grip. I reached for my compact, and in the mirror I saw Winnie. Her crooked, French-style baby bangs like an inmate's at the asylum. They barely extended an inch down her forehead, framing her face. I cried out a little. Tongue stared at the hair in his hand. He looked as though he wanted to find a way to glue it back on.

"Perfect," I said. "Drop that shit."

"Perfect?"

"I fucking love it."

And he threw the hair on the 160-year-old grave.

4

The mechanical bull in the corner was out of order—rusted to rat shit. But that didn't stop Tongue from trying to ride it. He mounted the beast and began to buck. His tree-trunk legs dwarfed the contraption. They dangled down to the pistachio-shell- and beer-piss-covered floor of the bar and flailed in an attempt to spur the make-believe monster into motion.

"Yip! Yip!"

I was on my fifth whiskey sour at the bar, and starting to see the walls crawl. The place was a hole, but the alcohol was cheap, and I was broke and thirsty. Hungry too. The bartender, Dewar, set down two bison burgers in front of me, and I started to gorge myself on red meat, hoping not to find a stray pubic hair in the flesh, for the kitchen was notorious. I was pretty sure they ran a cut-rate prostitution ring in the back. If not, surely someone regularly had their genitals out near the grill.

"Hey, Tex!"

Tongue dismounted and barrelled towards me. He

had been hesitant to come inside at first. He wanted to stay outside in the parking lot and chase after a flock of seagulls, but he'd lost all inhibitions after playing a few rounds of darts. I thought he'd surely put someone's eye out, and I hoped he would have too. The bull sealed the deal. Tongue was having a good time.

He took his place beside me and picked up his burger with one hand. The meal looked like a baseball inside his catcher's mitt. He stuffed it into his mouth, puffing hard through his nose. It made my eyes water and stomach turn looking at him eat. Grease ran, quivering, from the corners of his mouth. He was devouring the thing. Eyes wide open, swallowing. I could tell he just wanted to get back to his ride. I knew he could ravage anything he wanted to. I looked away for fear that he would inhale me next if I made eye contact. He could lap up and consume the whole place if he locked his jaw onto it. He was savage. Tongue would set to work on the tables and chairs next. He'd hoover down the unbalanced billiards table and all the balls. He'd suck back all the liquor, all the glassware, the waitresses, the bar backs, Dewar, the degenerates in their pathetic red plush booths, the vintage *Pac-Man* game in the corner, and the entire kitchen, slop buckets and all. Tongue would fit it all inside his glorious mouth and swallow. And I bet he would if I asked him to. His bison burger disappeared, and he licked the ketchup from his fingers, wiping them on his pants, and returned to his gyrations on the bull.

I've never been a fussy eater. I eat when I'm able to. Growing up, there was no such thing as breakfast, lunch, and dinner. Food would be around or it wouldn't be. And never really at a table. The idea seemed strange to me, actually. The only times I can remember sitting down to eat were when my mother would wake up momentarily from her endless sleep, worried that her children were malnourished, which we were. She'd force my brothers and me down at a table and put out two bowls: one loaded with ground beef and the other with turnips. We probably had a screaming match. I can't be certain. I do remember my brother Pete crying. His tears salted the bowl of meat.

Still, I could usually eat if I wanted to. My appetite followed the pattern of my latest escape. It's easy to stay trapped. People live their whole lives rewriting history and reinventing their prison sentence, just so they don't call it a jail cell. I'd always assumed that when my old man finally kicked off, I'd gain a hundred pounds from feasting on relief. The greatest of all escapes. But sitting there in front of my bison burger at Tongue's rodeo, I had lost any appetite. Maybe it was seeing Tongue maw down, or maybe it was the bitter taste of turnips that had suddenly turned up in my mouth. Either way, I was certainly glad not to have lost my thirst. I pushed away my plate of meat and ordered another whiskey sour.

I recognized the sound of Dirk's sinuses well before he slunk his way beside me at the bar. He had this horrible way of sucking in his snot and choking it back. It wasn't just a constant sniffle. The man was all leak. He reeked of mold and peppermints. Jittery as fuck.

"Hiya." Snort.

"What is it, Dirk?" I asked without looking up.

"Heee—" Choke.

Between his imploding loogies, Dirk would be giggling. I think it was a giggle. It was some kind of wet stammer that the son of a bitch couldn't control.

"S-s-so your dad's dead, eh?"

"You don't say."

"S-s-sorry." Giggle. Stammer. Belch.

"Have a burger, Dirk."

And he needed one desperately. He was a deformed, dying tree: curling stick arms and bow legs. A snivelling scarecrow pecked to shit by a flock of shit-ass birds.

"Yeah? Y-y-you done with 'er?"

"Sure." And I pushed the bison in front of him.

He had a bad case of the shakes, and it was exhausting to watch him try to steady the thing enough to take a bite. Just as he made to put it in his pathetic mouth, I asked him what he wanted.

"So?"

The question startled him, and with great pains, he put the burger back down without getting a bite. "S-s-saw you back at the funeral, b-b-but you left before I c-c-could talk...."

"Oh yeah?"

"Yeah."

Uncle Dirk had always been the most art-art-art-articulate in the family. He'd worked as a mail sorter at the post office for twenty-five years, but old Dirk had always longed to be given his own route. And why shouldn't he be? What did it matter that he was addicted to cough syrup and nudie magazines, that he would eat his scabs and was caught peeping in the ladies' washroom numerous times? He pleaded with his superiors, but either they couldn't figure out what he was saying or they never trusted him to actually interact with people. Best to keep the Dirks of the world underground. One day, he was reluctantly asked to fill in for one of the open-air carriers, and Dirk got himself run over by a Buick. He was being chased by a pack of the neighbourhood dogs and didn't see the car backing up. The driver left him in pieces on the pavement. He managed to escape the impact without any broken bones, but the dogs had at him on the ground, and that's why Dirk has only one ear.

"I been been been been.... I been...."

He was stammering up a bloody storm, forever shell-shocked by the wolf attack. I let him struggle.

"So I been been been been.... He ack ack ack ack...."

I was happy to have Dirk that way: quivery, runny camel spit. He was the spitting image of my father, minus about a hundred pounds. It was clear to me in that moment that the two were spawned from the same degenerate seed, and I would let this spastic phantom of my old man wriggle like a worm a child finds on the sidewalk on a spring morning after a rainfall and steps on just to watch the contortions play out on the concrete.

Dirk eventually gave up trying to string a sentence together. He reached into his pocket and produced a set of keys on a worn copper keychain—a cheesy-looking bird, a hawk. They belonged to my father.

"Henrietta!" Dirk finally coughed up.

That was the name of my father's limousine. It was his pride and joy. That's why he named it after my grandmother. He had started out driving a truck but never actually owned his own rig. He won Henrietta in a card game and started up his own business: Big Ben's Executive Fleet. Of course, Henrietta was the only ship in the fleet, and my father wore black track pants with his wrinkled tuxedo shirt and ill-fitting bow tie, but there were only a few limo companies in Oshawa, so he got a fair amount of work. Mostly weddings, proms, funerals, and whenever the Red Rooster Tavern booked him as the runner-up prize in their rib-eating contest.

"What about it?" I asked.

"Been asked by Big Bin...ah, Big Ben asked me... been begged by Big Bim.... Damnit. I. Been. Asked. By. Big. Ben...t-t-to give ya Henrietta." Dirk licked his lips with pride, for he'd carried out his charge at long last. He handed me the keys and went back to the burger.

Really, I wanted to stuff the hawk keychain up into Dirk's ear hole. I couldn't imagine why my father would leave me the stretched piece of shit, and if it was to alleviate any guilt he may have mustered in his dying days, I certainly didn't want to indulge it.

"Why not give it to one of the boys?" I asked, although I knew better.

Dirk opened his eyes wide in response and curled his bottom lip. He didn't know.

"I don't want the fucking thing," I said, throwing the keys down. They landed in Dirk's bowl of nuts. I threw a few crumpled bills down on the bar and headed out. Dirk must have been torn between finishing the bison and hunting for the hawk in the bowl because I was halfway across the parking lot when he emerged from the hellhole and caught up with me.

"C'mon, c'mon, take 'em," Dirk was pleading. He had my burger in one hand and the keys in the other. I was more bugged than drunk, but either way, I felt my heart racing, which was enough for me to know that I didn't know how I wanted to play this. Pride be damned, I was broke. I thought about how I could sell the thing. But I'd most likely just end up driving it off a cliff.

"B-B-Big Ben said," Dirk continued. "P-p-please take 'em. She's still in t-t-tip-top."

My indecision was marked by heavy breathing and what felt like a panic attack rising from my ankles. The episode was pierced, however, by strange high-pitched bird calls or sex cries. You can never be certain in that part of the city. Especially at that time of night, when the factories are letting out and the creek by the train tracks is crawling with desperate teenagers exploring the woods and their malnourished bodies. Dirk and I went around the other side of the plaza to investigate.

We found Tongue, still clad in his white suit, standing on top of Henrietta with his arms outstretched like the seagulls that flew around scavenging for French fries and puddles of ice cream cones in the parking lot. Tongue's girth was sinking in the roof of my father's pride and joy.

"Git the f-fuck down!" Dirk was ready to defend my father's honour, but I wasn't.

"Give me the keys, Dirk." I grabbed them from his gnarled hand. In the exchange, I must have jostled my chewed-up uncle, for he dropped the bison burger to the ground. A flurry of gulls descended on the meat, sending Dirk running for cover with one hand protecting his good ear.

I looked up at Tongue. I hadn't intended on taking him to an amusement park, but a huge, stupid grin was flashing teeth and gums more pink than a cloud of cotton candy.

"You ever been in a limo before?" I asked the giant still standing on the roof. His shadow blocked the glare of filthy orange neon.

"No way." Tongue was on the verge of taking flight.

"Get down and get in," I told him. He did, and we took our places inside that stale, smoky leather cab. I figured I could at least give Tongue a joy ride before driving it off a cliff. It took me a minute to adjust the mirrors. It was hard to judge distances while high, and especially so in old, elongated Henrietta. As we peeled away, I just barely managed to avoid backing into Dirk, now fighting off the gulls for a morsel of food.

5

Driving drunk in that dead man's car. Above me, the woolly mammoth howled through the moon roof at the deserted dead-end streets where stray cats and glue-sniffing turpentine freaks staggered about waiting for the bars to let out. I was wild coming down off the day. I hadn't been in the limo since I was fifteen years old. That New Year's Eve I stole Dad's keys and went drinking down by the airport with my eighteen-year-old boyfriend Trevor. He was a senior in high school who always wore a black trench coat and let me paint his fingernails different colours. He thought it made him look cool, and I like that he thought that. I knew the rainbow effect made him look like an arsehole, which he was. But old enough to buy beer and modestly employed at the bowling alley, he'd bring me booze and steal the size-six shoes the bowlers traded in for bowling shoes whenever I wanted.

We rang in the new year in an empty, pathetic patch of field parked beside a hangar that housed two or three small Cessna planes. Trev had written me more bad poetry, and I just laughed and laughed at him as the ball dropped. I did appreciate the red high heels he'd snagged and told him to stick to stealing shoes instead of verses from shitty punk bands, and this made him pout most of the night. It was a good thing, I suppose, because we had originally driven down to the airport with the intention of stealing a two-seater plane and flying it away from our prison. His hissy fit meant that neither of us would have to make excuses for not going through with it, neither one of us wanting to admit that we'd lost the nerve. We eventually made up and had teenage sex instead. I'm pretty sure that was the night I got pregnant, but I can't be certain. The airport was actually the local military training base for peewee reserves, and some volunteer sergeant found us under Trev's trenches and pages of poetry and reported us. When my father woke up, already a week into the new year, he sent his hounds, my brothers, after Trevor, and I never heard from him again. I don't remember missing him much, but my collection of shoes soon dwindled, and I started painting my kid brother's nails instead.

It started to rain, but Tongue didn't seem to care. He was getting whipped and slapped around up there, but it only made him howl harder. I worried that I wouldn't ever be able to get rid of him, really, for I was already sobering up enough to know that I could take only so much of this, that I needed to get out for good and that he couldn't come with me.

I needed a cigarette but didn't have any smokes. With one hand on the wheel to keep Henrietta steady through those drowned-rat streets, I reached around the front seat, hoping to find something to smoke. I tried the glovebox. Out popped a rolled-up porno magazine from the seventies with the cover model standing backwards bent at the waist, her hair dangling to the ground. The title ASS was written in red block letters. I reached in past a stack of unpaid parking tickets and found a cigar box. My father used to keep cigars on hand to sell to his passengers for fifteen dollars each. He said they were Cubans, but the box had Portuguese writing on it, and he used to buy them for fifty cents each at Mike's Variety downtown. I placed the box on the seat next to me.

"Hey," I called up to Tongue in the wind.

"Ho!" He continued to hold his arms straight up in the air towards the moon.

"You want a smoke?"

"Nope."

"They're Cubans."

"Where?"

I couldn't get Tongue to come out of the rain. I flipped up the lid of the wannabe Cubans, and, as if jumping out at me like oversized confetti, stacks of one hundred dollar bills burst forth out of that box. I slammed on the breaks. Henrietta came to a reckless, screeching halt as Tongue, a human cannonball, shot straight out of the moon roof and soared in front.

My heart raced now as I scanned the street, my

hands clutching the steering wheel. I felt sick waiting for him to land. But he never did. I quickly stuffed the money back inside the box and forced the lid closed, then jammed the treasure underneath the driver's seat and staggered out of the limo.

"Hey! Where are you? Are you okay?"

I wondered if I'd launched him to the fucking moon, because there was no sign of him anywhere. No sound beyond my own pulse, which I heard like a sick propeller in my chest.

"Christ! Are you okay?"

I really didn't want to stumble upon him dead in the street. And if he'd survived the impact on the pavement, I figured it would be like finding a beached whale. I'd have to wake up the entire block to help hoist him back inside the limo. I pictured Tongue splattered across the street with hard rain washing him away into the gutter. I began to cry big fat tears. I was shaking now. I didn't even know his real name. Constantine? Tongue?

"Billy!" I called out. "Billy, where the fuck are you?"

A few lights started to come on in the shitty little windows of those shitty little post-war A-frame houses that stood crooked on Athol Street. I could feel eyes peering out at me searching for Tongue in the storm, but no one dared step out of their caves to help me look. The sight of Henrietta probably made me look like some kind of messed-up bride on her wedding night, starting her domestic disputing early.

"Jesus, Billy. Jesus Christ."

I wanted to be washed away too. Or to look up to find Tongue orbiting the moon. A flash of lightning streaked across the sky and momentarily lit up the night. And though lightning bolts usually die out as quickly as they come alive, this one seemed to linger just above the earth, and I saw a stark white brilliance beaming in the front yard of one of the houses. I ran towards it.

It was Tongue's white suit about twenty feet in the air. He was wrapped around the trunk of a huge maple. His arms and legs strangled the tree, and his face was pressed hard against the bark. It was the first time I'd seen the creature scared.

"What the hell, man? Get down out of that tree."

Tongue looked down at me briefly, then redoubled his cling and pressed his face flat against the tree. It looked as though he were talking to it or licking it, maybe chewing on the damn thing.

"Come on down, now!" He didn't look hurt, but I couldn't be certain.

Tongue mouthed the words *help me* and looked down in my direction again.

"Hold on."

I raced back to Henrietta and drove over to Tongue's perch. Then, hopping the car up onto the curb, I parked as close as I could underneath him. I climbed into the back seat and shimmied up through the still-open moon roof.

"Jump down."

Tongue surveyed the scene. Henrietta's roof, which had once filled him with such delight, he now regarded with great mistrust. I pounded on the wet metal.

"Get down here now, man. It's not that far." But it was.

Tongue landed with a thud, and I just managed to slink back inside the car before he could crush me. The sky had fallen. I pulled at his soaking wet white suit, and he poured back into Henrietta and stretched out on his back. I closed up the moon roof, climbed back to the front seat, and drove off.

I was completely sober now, and certain realizations began to sink in. First, I was starting to care for this monster. I found myself continuously looking back in the rear-view mirror to check up on him. He was shivering slightly with his eyes closed. Second, and most important, I was sitting on at least twenty thousand dollars.

Not accepting Henrietta was one thing. I could do without her, and I would gladly reject her if it meant I could savour the spite. But to reject the money would be idiotic. Until now, I didn't have enough cash to buy a stick of gum.

Tongue began to moan in his sleep. I think it was moaning. There was a little too much melody to it to be sure but not enough rhythm to it to be a song. I wondered if he had broken any bones, but I was convinced now that he was all rubber. Still, I decided it best to get him checked out.

6

At that time of night, the triage waiting room is always filled with a kind of heightened terror. I knew it well. There's something about suffering in the middle of the night when the rest of the world sleeps that makes people feel all the more sorry for themselves. Maybe it's because the hospital is one of the only places that's open late and so there are no other public places for people to go to lick their wounds in front of an audience.

Of the thirteen or so afflicted in the room, there were only one or two real sufferers. The old guy in the stretcher, sucking back oxygen from a mask—he was bad. The fifteen-year-old girl as white as a ghost, doubled up in pain and arms clutching her gut—she was bad. And the young mother who had finally run out of tears from bawling ever since they took in her kid who had a split skull—she was bad too. But the rest of them were nowhere near it. Pathetic snifflers watched infomercials on a TV in the corner. Some arsehole with a sprained ankle kept getting up and limping, all drama, to the nurses' station to see if he was next. I felt like the pill popper in the corner: numb.

I couldn't tell if Tongue had agreed to go because he too thought that he might be hurt or because he was just up for another outing and didn't want our adventures to end. He seemed fine. Still wet and still shaking but happy to be eating a candy bar I'd bought for him from a buzzing vending machine. Tongue was glued to the television.

I had taken the box of hundreds in with me and held onto it as if it contained the soul of some Portuguese wizard, or at least his last dying breath.

"Hang back," I said to Tongue. "Going to the washroom." Tongue looked blankly at me with chocolate-smeared lips.

I locked myself in a stall and sat down on the edge of the toilet. For a hospital, the washroom seemed like a health hazard. It was filthy. I didn't care. I opened up my treasure chest and started organizing the bills so that I could count. I was nearing seventy-five when I lost track upon hearing the washroom door squeak open. I instinctively lifted my feet so that they couldn't be seen through the opening below the door of the stall.

"Anybody in here?" It was a man's voice. "Hello? Cleaner."

I heard him wheel in some kind of cart and lock the door behind him. I balanced the cigar box and the yet-to-be-counted money on my lap as my thighs began to ache from their awkward position in mid-air. I prayed he'd be quick in his duties, and considering the state of the wreckage around me, he didn't seem to be too diligent a worker. But as he rummaged around, I knew he had other business. I heard the beeping of his cell phone.

"Baby? Hey, baby. Yeah. No, I know.... Whatcha thinking? I got 'em. Yeah, same as last time, I think. What? Hold up. Lemme check." He began to rummage around again inside his scrubs. I longed for him to fuck off. I was a hostage now on that toilet seat, held ransom by the blood money in my lap. I heard the rattling of pills, and he started to whisper, "*Ibru*something. *Ibru-pro-fen.* I got, like, nine bottles of the shit. Huh? What do you mean?"

The imbecile had snagged himself a whack of over-the-counter garbage. I took heart in that at least, but I still wished him dead. I must have inadvertently laughed because he was suddenly silent.

"Hello? Someone there?"

I held my breath, but he was onto me and started banging on all the stalls.

In times of capture, it's best to play dead. Or so I was taught in my grade five geography class when we were preparing to take a camping trip. We watched this grainy 16 mm film on how to survive in the outdoors. My teacher must not have screened the film beforehand because it wasn't appropriate for children. Besides the usual directions on how to start a fire, the best places to bury your shit, and how to pitch a tent, the archaic guide had multiple references to cannibalism and bear attacks. Play dead. The reenactments were so lifelike that the entire class reported having nightmares to their parents, and the trip was cancelled.

Nightmares weren't new for me, but I too was affected by the film. A recurring dream had me being pursued in a field of monstrous sunflowers. The creature after me—nameless, faceless—would be close. I knew he was near from his breathing, which was always loud and hot like a furnace, an unrelenting wave of bad breath. I'd invariably stumble, and for fear of the attack, I'd play dead. But in my dreams, playing dead didn't keep him off. If anything, he wanted me that way: docile, compliant, quiet, unmoving.

"Get the fuck out of here!" I screamed this at the guy on the other side of my cage. My shrieking startled him enough that he dropped his stolen pills. I heard the bottles smack against the sticky tiles. Then he scrabbled at the door, pulling his cart, and he was gone.

I bolted up off the toilet spastically, and a pile of money went flying. Some landed in the disgusting bowl below. I reached in past my gagging and pulled out the wet bills and shook them off. Once out of the stall, I just couldn't let good, albeit inferior, painkillers go to waste and so collected them too. The scene was all smeared in pissy waters, and I was filthy, but I held some kind of sick pride inside as I glimpsed my rugged face with my demented bangs in the mirror. I knew this terrain well, and it was more than just mere survival; I was thriving and rich.

I steadied up. Turned on the faucet and ran some of the really shitty bills under the water. Turned on the hand dryer. Hot air blew hard, and I waved around the dripping wad of filthy cash. Dirty money. Dirtier now. Could never be cleaned. It was impossible to think that my father had given me the dough as a form of reconciliation, and even if he had, I rejected that notion. I reject forgiveness. But I could still reason my way around taking it. Standing in that disease-ridden washroom, drying out the loot, I did it like so: The money was just another of my father's cruel challenges. He was the kind of man who enjoyed watching others fail because he himself was a total failure. As such, he got off on setting you up for disaster.

When my brother Pete was six, he wanted a puppy. He wanted a puppy more than anything in the world, and instead of just saying no because our house was already a human zoo and we couldn't afford any more inmates, one day my father showed up with this mangy, half-dead-looking cockatoo he called Scuzzy. He told Pete to take extra special care of Scuzzy because Scuzzy was an extra special bird—so special that he couldn't fly. I swear to God that the old bastard must have clipped Scuzzy's wings. And the very next day, my father showed up at the house with this raccoon. Except he said it was a cat he found hunting for fish bones in the alley. He said he looked so unhappy that he just had to take him home. Dad called the "cat" Boner. Dad chained Boner to his easy chair in the living room and told us that we couldn't feed him because he didn't want us to get attacked by his razor-sharp claws.

Pete woke up that night the way we all did, hearing screeching coming from the living room. Scuzzy's cage was on the floor next to my father's chair, and the bird was in spasm, wriggling around, croaking because Boner was baring his teeth and clawing at the cage.

"What ya gonna do, boy?" My father was drunk, yes, but he had surely devised this freak show in his waking moments of sobriety. "You gonna save old Scuzzy? Boner's gonna eat old Scuzzy unless you can save him." My father was howling.

What hurt me most was watching my older brothers' initial terror turn to delight as the tension mounted. Soon they were all over by my father, joining in on the taunting. My little brother Pete stood paralyzed by the door, looking from my father to Scuzzy to Boner and back to Scuzzy again. He started bawling, and he peed himself. He was wearing one-piece Batman pyjamas, and a wet spot formed in the front.

My father only redoubled his efforts: "C'mon! You gonna cry and piss yourself or are you gonna save Scuzzy?" Then my father went over and opened up the tiny door on the bird's cage. "Boner's a-hungry. Boner's a-hungry." Then he went over to the killer raccoon and started to jangle his chain. Rattling it. My older brothers roared with fear and delight.

Now, I'd like to believe that I didn't join in on the goading. I choose to believe this, but I can't be certain. Either way, Pete just continued to piss and cry until my father had enough and unchained the raccoon so that the animal was free to ravage the bird. Of course, years later he'd denied this tale of horror as another of my fool inventions. He'd said I dreamed it up. That it never happened. It was true that I often saw the man morph into different kinds of rodents, but Boner, the raccoon, was real. My father had used him to teach Pete that he wasn't ready or able to look after a pet. We were meant to accept failure, usually in the form of carnage, as the norm, as if somehow, without the presence of feathers and blood, screeching, nails on orange shag carpet, we weren't confronting life head-on. The way he did. The way he did when Pete swallowed a golf ball on a schoolyard dare and choked to death.

That was the perfect lesson in failure for our family, and we responded by never mentioning Pete's name again. We erased him when we buried him in that shoebox coffin. I choose to believe that I didn't participate in that sick practice, however. That I cried myself to sleep many nights thinking about him. That I have spoken his name at least once in the past fifteen years. But who knows? When history is repeatedly reinvented in order to bear the weight of the present, the mind becomes a kind of mudslide where the muck runs fast beneath your feet. And anyway, I'm saying his name now: Pete.

I was standing in a puddle of awful in that washroom, counting bills and thinking this way. Wondering what my father had intended by all of this. I was rich. How on earth the son of a bitch managed to get his hands on twenty-three thousand dollars, I didn't know, but by the time I'd reached the bottom of the cigar box, the ground shifted. The real trap was stuck to the bottom. It was a picture of a newborn baby. The infant was tightly wrapped in blue hospital linens. His tiny features were wrinkled and slightly swollen. A grouchy newborn who hadn't asked to be born. As if God had sat on his face. So it was a trap after all. I bundled up the twenty-three grand and cradled it in my arms. Popped a handful of the cheap painkillers and kicked open the door. I accepted my father's challenge.

Tongue wasn't in the waiting room when I got back. I was glad they'd taken him in finally. It meant I wouldn't have to say goodbye. He was in the hands of those more capable. I did feel a twinge of something for just leaving him there, but I had to get out. Every orderly in sight was staring daggers into me, and the place was crawling with failure. I hurried past the groaning group in the waiting room and headed towards the exit with the automatic revolving doors.

"Oh, Miss," a nurse called to me as I stepped out into the night, but I knew better than to look back. "Excuse me. Excuse me, Winnie?" I almost didn't recognize my new name. The nurse was pushing Tongue in a wheelchair. He was wrapped up in an enormous blue blanket.

"Just came out for a smoke," I muttered.

"Will you be driving Constantine home tonight?" she asked. She took out a bottle of pills and handed them to me. "He's sustained a mild concussion. He really shouldn't be climbing trees in a thunderstorm. Especially with his condition."

I wondered what he'd told her.

"Which condition is that?" I asked. Did the survival guide warn against the dangers of big tongues acting as lighting rods?

"He can't sustain a fall given the fact that his fontanel is exposed."

"His what?"

"Constantine's fontanel, the soft spot on the top of his head. It never closed. A more common condition than you might imagine."

"S'true," Tongue said. "Fontanel never closed."

"Open for business, eh?" I said.

"That's not the important bit," the nurse continued. "What matters tonight is that he stay awake for at least ten hours and that he drink plenty of water. Danger signs will exhibit in the form of cold sweats, fever, shakes, vomiting, drowsiness. There's a slight chance that he may slip into a coma, but the doctor feels that he's well enough to go home as long as you keep an eye on him."

She began helping Tongue to his feet. I cringed. Faker, I thought. The nurse stayed with Tongue while I went to get the limo. I pulled up to the hospital entrance.

"Ooh la la, so fancy!" The nurse was excited to see Henrietta. "That's first class, eh?"

Tongue got in the front beside me. I gave him my father's tattered chauffeur's hat.

"For your open dome," I told him.

Then we drove off.

7

I knew I couldn't wait the ten hours to keep the galoot from swallowing his tongue, so we stopped in at a twenty-four-hour doughnut shop, and I plied him with two extra large coffees and a box of fried lard, hoping that the sugar, fat, and caffeine would do the trick.

After I fed him, I said, "I'm gonna have to drop you off at your place now 'cause I gotta get going." Tongue was grazing on a bear claw—the last of a baker's dozen.

"You feeling okay?"

"Don't know."

"I gotta get going," I insisted.

"Where?" he asked me. Despite the dough in his throat and that bulging muscle working hard in his mouth, I heard his words clearly.

"Don't know," I said. He seemed to understand. In fact, he always seemed to understand no matter how warped I came across. He didn't ask many questions. Never made me explain myself. I prefer things that way. "So I'll drop you off at your place, but you have to stay awake until tomorrow, okay?"

"'Kay," Tongue agreed. But by the time we pulled up to the ice cream parlour, he was already fading on me.

"Hey!" I snapped my fingers. "You can't fall asleep."

"Resting..." he muttered.

"Don't. Keep your eyes open. If you fall asleep, you may not wake up." Tongue laughed at the idea. Endless sleep did seem like a beautiful thought, but I repeated myself just to be clear. "Don't go to sleep. Don't close your eyes. Watch a movie or something. I gotta get going."

I felt uneasy leaving him there—a drowsy bear with a hole in his head. It wasn't going to be easy for me to erase him. Even though I'd only known him for a couple of days, he'd be tough to snuff out. My chest felt tight the second he disappeared inside his den. And tighter still as I drove away and pulled into the gas station a few blocks from his place. But I knew any hint of guilt was just failure, compassion, a weakness that I couldn't afford to indulge in.

I tried to push the feeling away while I filled Henrietta up with high-grade gasoline and bought a few cartons of cigarettes. The jerky clerk behind the counter made a big production over the hundred dollar bill I paid with. As he fussed with the money, holding it up to the light to verify that it was real, the thought suddenly crossed my mind that Dad's lesson may end up being much crueller and shorter-lived than I first assumed...but the bill checked out. It was real. All of it. And it was all mine.

Gasoline and cigarettes would be my sole means of survival now. I figured I could do without most things and people. I certainly knew that I'd need to try to stay sober from now on behind the wheel. Driving drunk was fine in the 'Shwa, but there would be no way I could endure a long road trip if I were messed up all the time.

I opened a pack of smokes and reached for the lighter in my pocket. I found Tongue's pills, and once again it was hard for me to breathe. It should have been a win, as they looked like some pretty heavy-duty shit, but my joints were turning into jelly. I couldn't deny it. Not that I thought that he needed them. It was just that his goddamn kindness had ensnared me somehow. I cared about him now in my own way, and I couldn't shake this compulsion to see him through the night. I did an about-face, begrudgingly, and headed back to Tongue's.

I let myself in the main entrance and walked up the long, narrow stairwell. I knocked on the door. "Hey, Billy. I'm back." I pressed my face against the door, convinced that the oaf had not listened to me and had fallen asleep. I pounded harder. "Hey! Open up." I heard a dog barking from an upstairs room. Trying the knob, I found the door unlocked and pushed my way in.

The TV was on, showing a late-night program on catfish. The white suit was heaped in a pile in the kitchen. I found Tongue lying naked in his giant bed. His mouth was open like a sewer hole. The dead pink thing moist and protruding. A whale trying to swallow a moose. There was certainly nothing small about this man. I admit that I marvelled at his huge cock and balls for a moment before my wonder turned into panic and I had to look away. I covered his exposed genitals with a pillow.

"Hey.... Hey, wake up!" I started clapping my hands, but I knew I'd have to touch him. I knelt beside his splayed body and began pushing on his solid chest. It was like pushing into wet mud, supple earth. I bounced him up and down with an increasing rhythm. "Hey, hey, hey, hey!" He was hard to move, and I wasn't sure if it was because of how tiny I was beside the sleeping walrus or because he'd slipped into a fucking coma. I started slapping his face, hard. I was sitting on his chest now, screaming into the goddamn hole in his head. "Wake up! Get up! Hey!" I lost control of my breathing. I rested my knees against his shoulders and tried to lift his massive head. His tongue slipped inside his open mouth, and he smiled before opening his eyes. I stopped and panted above him. Felt as though I'd wrestled with an alligator.

"Winnie." He stared at me. There was a hint of cruelty in his eyes, or maybe there wasn't. Had he been pretending? Playing dead? Whether he had intended to or not, he had scared me, and I felt vulnerable sitting high on top of the naked mountain.

I grabbed his face in my hands. "Billy! Don't do that."

He started to laugh, moving the mountain beneath me, and I climbed off, hiking down my skirt.

"You forgot your pills," I said.

Tongue stood up, rubbing his cheeks, which had gone a bright pink from my repeated blows. He didn't care that he was naked. Why should I?

"I told you not to fall asleep. I can't stay, so where can I take you so that you won't fall asleep?" I wished there was some tank of cold water that I could put him in. Let him stay suspended for a few hours. Float it off. "Don't you have any family who can take you in for a few days? Anybody?"

It seemed like a demeaning question, and it was. I disgusted myself, but I felt that if I didn't leave the city that night, my entire escape would be compromised. I'd already wasted an hour. Tongue, who had enjoyed getting such a rise out of me, began to pout. It was clear that he didn't want me to go. What made it worse was that he refused to say it. He refused to ask me to stay. He never asked for anything.

Finally, he said, "Take me to Mama's then."

"Your mother's house?" I don't know why I was surprised that he had a mother. I suppose I hadn't considered any woman being able to give birth to such a creature. I suppose I'd imagined that Tongue had just hatched that way one day.

"Yeah, take me to Mama's."

"Okay, let's go." I felt invigorated. "Put on some clothes. Maybe pack a bag in case you need to stay longer." I tried to hurry him along. I found a duffle bag in the hall closet and began to load in his wardrobe. I'd never seen so much flannel. I was also impressed by his extensive collection of wool socks—all mismatched and holey and huge with the elastics worn out. I stuffed everything into the bag.

"Where do you keep your underwear?" I asked him.

"I don't," he said. "Never wear 'em."

I gathered up some blankets too and his pills and his normal-sized toothbrush. Tongue lagged behind. I couldn't tell if he was just moping or if he was showing warning signs. I couldn't tell if he was acting stranger than normal. I suppose I was flustered because I'd come back and seen his junk and touched his face. He was stuck to the TV, watching some hillbilly catch a fish by having the thing jump up and glom onto his arm.

"Let's go," I insisted. Tongue rose laboriously and reluctantly stepped into his boots barefoot. I gave him the bag and slapped him on the back a few times. "Buck up, Billy. It's for the best." I had been afraid to touch him at first, but there was something about the electric shockwave radiating up my arm that gave me strength.

In the stairwell, I asked, "So where does Mama live?"

"Downstairs," he said.

8

Mama lived in a moldy old backroom behind the ice cream parlour. It wasn't just her in there either. I assumed we'd be tiptoeing into a sleeping scene at that hour, but when Tongue opened the door, the place was buzzing with activity. First off, it smelled like shit. Well, cabbage, I think. There was an oversized pot on the stove bubbling up something awful and sending plumes of steam into the air. Some comatose man was wheezing in an armchair in front of an old television set with the volume up full, the pictured scrambled, flickering strange blue shadows throughout the dimly lit hovel. A spastic kid about seven or eight years old, lost in its own world, wearing a pair of toy rabbit ears and talking to itself in different voices, was drawing in chalk on the walls.

Mama hurried over when she saw us and immediately took the duffle bag from Tongue and started searching inside it. She was a brick of a lady with thick arms and legs. Her ankles were swollen to the size of paint cans. She had varicose veins like crawling vines.

She wore a muumuu, perfectly square and deep navy blue. As wide as she was tall. Spoke in a kind of whining barnyard drawl. It wasn't English. At least I hoped it wasn't. Maybe Russian? She refused to look at me and seemed to be chiding Tongue for something he either did or didn't do. I looked to him for a translation.

"Mama wanna know if I made you pregnant."

I howled, but the devil in her eyes told me to stop, so I did. She meant business. She must have thought I was Tongue's lover. She kept on him with the brute babble, flapping her arms around, clucking like a frantic fucking hen.

"I'm not his woman," I said as clearly as I could without laughing. "Me. No baby." I shook my head and patted my belly. "No hank-pank." I pointed to the huge bulge in Tongue's pants.

Mama froze and regarded me from the corner of her cataracts. I did manage to silence her some. I just needed to let her in on Tongue's condition so that I could leave guilt-free.

"Tell her about the concussion," I said to Tongue.
"Can't."
"Why not?"
"Won't listen."
"She deaf?"
"Mad."
"Well, tell her I'm not pregnant."
"I did."
"So...."

"It's the garbage."

Mama scurried off and came back with two large black garbage bags. I swear to God they were the same size as she was. She threw them at our feet.

"What's this?" I asked Tongue. "You were supposed to take out the trash?"

Tongue seemed scared. It was alarming to see the command the old battle-axe held over this giant. Mama was raising holy hell. I was determined to end it. Although she was a terror, I wasn't afraid of her. Not yet anyway. I picked up the bags to take them outside. Mama immediately lunged for them, so I let go. She fell to the ground, guarding her garbage. Three piles lay by our feet now.

"What's this all about? For Christ's sake."

As Tongue reached down to scoop up Mama, the kid in bunny ears came lurching over to me. I couldn't tell if it was a he or a she. The thing was sexless and freckled to shit, and it wore a cast around its pelvis, which made it walk mechanically. The child stood, legs splayed, teetering.

"I know, I know, I know," it said in a breathless squeak. "Mama's angry tonight! Mama's angry tonight!"

"Why's that?"

"Oh, oh, oh, I know, I know." The child was all insect.

"Spill it," I told it.

"Vlad lost her pearls again, the big ones from Objuck. Mama's angry!"

I was trying to understand, but I needed more to go on. At the sound of Vlad's name, Mama pounded her fist into her other meat-mitt hand. She was damning this Vlad to hell. Then she began to yell at the garbage bags again. Tongue stood frozen in the middle. His head down, face slack—a melting wax candle.

"Is this Vlad?" I asked, and went over to the man sprawled in the flea-bitten armchair in the corner. It was death: an old man with his head tilted back, his mouth open, as were his eyes, which stared straight up at the ceiling. He had dust in his wrinkles.

"Who?" The child had a terrible way of picking at itself while it bobbed around, looking as if it needed to be hosed down.

"Him," I said, pointing to the seated collection of bones.

The child laughed spastically. Its entire body vibrating, shaking its head. Its googly eyes were about to pop out at any second. It laughed and laughed. Apparently, it was a stupid question. Tongue figured out what Mama was after at long last and slumped to the floor. Tore into the garbage bags by our feet. He started sorting through the trash, looking for Mama's pearls, I presumed.

"That's Objuck! Not Vlad! That's Objuck!" The child, like an excited praying mantis, leaped over to Objuck and sat down on his bony lap. The old man's eyes widened, and his mouth formed a painful, silent O. Then the insect started to pull on the old bastard's huge hairy ears. "She thought you were Vlad! Objuck! Objuck! She thought you were Vlad, Objuck! Can you believe it?"

Tongue was pulling up scraps from dinners past. Mostly vegetable scraps. But I also glimpsed scraps of bandage, diaper, and stained wrapping paper. The pot in the kitchen was bubbling over. Mama went to tend to it.

"I'm getting the hell out of here," I said to Tongue. I was standing over him, which felt strange. He looked up at me. Disgust washed over his tired face. "I'm not helping sort that crap. Where's Vlad? Get Vlad to do it if he lost the bloody pearls." Each time I uttered his name, Mama cursed out in Slavic barnyard.

"This is Objuck!" the child screamed again. "It's not Vlad!"

"Who the fuck is Vlad?"

A man appeared amid the chaos. He wore an apron over a hairy chest that showed specks of sweat and ice cream. His jet-black hair was greased back under a hairnet. He had a toothpick protruding from the right corner of his mouth and a cigarette dangling from the left.

"I am Vlad." He spoke in a slow sleaze—also animal but English.

"Who do you have, Constance? This is fine." He was referring to me, staring at my ass. "Name, please?"

"I'm Winnie," I said.

"Vinnie." He savoured my name on his lips. "Do you vant an extra large banana split, Vinnie dear? I give

— 63 —

you big fatty with cherry on top!" Then he licked some cream off his wrist. He found himself sexy. He laughed until it turned into a kind of coughing fit. He caught the phlegm, and his tone changed. Then he began to bark at Tongue on the ground, who had exhausted his search of the first bag and was well into the second mess. As Vlad shouted, he flicked Tongue's earlobe with his sticky fingers and then tapped him on the top of his head with his knuckle.

"That's Vlad!" The child bounded back to us. "That's him! Vlad! Now you know!"

As he came close, the caustic candyman snapped his fingers, and the child shut up. "Vhat is it, Mama? Pearls? Eh? I don't have."

Mama charged over, and the two of them had at each other. Fangs and fists—it was terrible, really. I tried to get my message out about Tongue needing to stay awake because of his injury, but my words were lost in the sound of mess. When I produced the pills, however, they both became quiet, and the two of them lunged for the bottle of painkillers. I dropped it in the pile of strewn garbage. They dropped to their knees, mother and son, and began to hunt for the pills, savagely.

Tongue stood up and stared at me. He was wearing the saddest face in the fucking world. I realized in that moment that Tongue too needed to escape. That all families are filled with madness, debt, loss, and rot, not just mine. That Tongue's own survival, which I'd never before considered, was contingent on his wonderful world of sugar and make-believe. But when the bitter harshness penetrates, and it always does, even Tongue would be forced back into the shitstorm of life.

"Objuck!" The child started screeching. "Objuck! No!"

I looked over to the dying man's perch, but he wasn't there.

"In here, in here, in here," the child continued.

Mama, Vlad, Tongue, and I pushed through the double doors that led into the ice cream parlour. Objuck was sprawled on the countertop. He had managed to wedge his entire skeletal frame inside the ice cream display freezer. He was shivering. His face was smeared with the colours of the rainbow. Butterscotch elbows and whippy running down his sunken chest. He buried his face deep inside a bucket of sweet cream light, and he started licking the shit out of it while humming some wild Russian folk song. Mama and Vlad struggled to disentangle the ancient man from the frozen flavours.

I took in the freak show for a good long moment. Then I said to Tongue, "Grab a pail for the road."

"Which flavour?" he asked, excited. "Vanilla or choco?"

"Doesn't matter. You choose. We gotta go."

Tongue grabbed one of each.

As we headed out, I looked back to see the crippled kid in the window, pulling out a long string of white

– 65 –

pearls from the pelvic cast. The beads appeared like a shining umbilical cord that strangled and wrapped around the kid's reaching fist.

9

The Trans-Canada Highway stretched out before us for hours. I had always measured time in distances, and so I hoped that the farther I could get away from the structures surrounding my former life, the further I'd be from my former self. I was already mapping out this emotional geography, and I found myself content in the middle of nowhere, although I knew that I'd been long since spread across this country, divided up into pieces like butchers' work, and at any turn I might come across a burial site or landmine that would pull me back. So, as much as I embraced the endless forest and drift of solemn trees crossing Ontario, I regarded the landscape with a kind of mistrust. I didn't let myself get taken in by the beauty of the bush. I preferred to keep my eyes fixed on the road before us. I figured that the only way to make it through alive was to press on, head-on into a directionless, futureless future and confront any nameless ghosts hiding in the wilderness. I was also high, so that helped.

Besides, we hadn't gotten that far away yet. Henrietta

was proving to be an untrustworthy bitch. She broke down a few times in the initial phases of our escape. To be safe, I'd kept Tongue awake by cranking the country music on the radio and giving him cola spiked with uppers. No matter the twang blaring through the speakers, Tongue sang along. He loved to sing. He fit the words *darling* and *honky-tonk* at the end of every verse of every crooning tune we heard speeding through the night. I found it endearing at first. For those first few hours, I laughed along. But as my ears began to bleed and the limo kept stalling on us and I saw that nothing would faze him, I began to fantasize about ripping out his tongue and hanging myself with it. I pushed away any regret I was feeling for bringing him along. New car rules stated that we would limit the country music station to one hour a day, and Tongue could only sing along to those tunes that he knew by heart. He was still free to gyrate all he wanted, and he did, non-stop sometimes.

At 4 a.m., in the middle of Tongue's yodeling sessions just outside of Ottawa, the limo began to sound like a dying moose. Then a truck loaded with teenagers pulled up beside us, honking and shooting fists into the air. "Rock on!" one of them shouted.

I looked in the rear-view mirror to see sparks coming off the ass end of Henrietta, leaving a jet stream of smoke in our wake. I pulled over, and Tongue and I went around to investigate. I didn't know much about cars, but I could see that the muffler, which was rusted through, was hanging down and had been scraping against the road. I wasn't sure how long we'd been dragging it, as the music had been blasting awhile.

"Muffler's fucked," I said.

Tongue agreed. Without saying a word, the honky-tonk man stretched himself out underneath the vehicle and started to mess with the burning-hot metal. He let out a scream that echoed through the surrounding forest.

"What is it?" I was used to his loud sounds by now, but I was on edge on the side of the highway.

"Hot!"

"No guff. Leave it. We'll find a place in the morning."

"Naw."

Tongue had fixed the car himself on the previous breakdowns and was happy to be of assistance. After all, what exactly would he be bringing to our trip? I had all the money, and I was doing all the driving. He continued to let out yelps as he worked at pulling off the muffler. It was wild watching him work, really. His huge legs protruded from underneath the car, and I thought then that he had the power to lift the entire thing off the ground if he wanted. He looked bigger than the limo anyway, clad in his white suit that needed a bath. Tongue started to rock the muffler up and down. As he did, Henrietta seemed to rise and fall at his mercy.

"You're gonna crush yourself."

When I went into the cab to retrieve some more electric soda, I heard the sound of a train crash. I looked back to see Tongue holding the snub-nosed shark in his arms with a look of pride on his goofy face.

"Ditch it," I told him.

Tongue pitched the sea creature to the side of the highway, and we continued on. But without a muffler, Henrietta now sent clouds of black smoke into the air, and no amount of country crooning would drown out her roar. She sounded like a tank bearing down on a target, and this only further enlivened local teenage hot-rodders as we blared through the back roads outside the nation's capital. The limo kept overheating too. I found us a cheap motel near a mechanic shop, and we pulled in for the night.

I'd spent many nights in similar dives. The place was aptly named "Get Some ZZZs," but the sign was partially burned out, so it simply read "Get Some." And by the look of the stained bed and the red bulbs in the lamps, many travellers had. The place was a typical truck stop. I knew them well since they had marked my entire summer vacation when I was twelve. That was the summer my family packed up inside Dad's rig to drive Mom down to the loony bin in New Brunswick. Of course, at the time, I didn't know any better. I thought we were going to fucking Disney World.

My brothers and I sat in the trailer. Although it was summer, we had to wear snowsuits because Dad was hauling a load of frozen meat, which meant that the freezer had to be kept on for the entire trip. I didn't know what was happening for most of the drive. Whenever we'd stop to pee, I'd catch a glimpse of

Mom crying or laughing in her sleep in the cab. I knew something was up because my eldest brother, Liam, was not his usual tyrannical self. He kept trying to get us to shut up in the back while he pressed his ear carefully against the chilly wall adjacent to the cab, trying to make out the deranged psychotic babbling coming from my parents.

The last I saw of my mother was the back of her head while two men in white ushered her into a huge manor house painted up in soft lime green. The air smelled of seaweed. Dad let us throw rocks at each other on the beach before we drove into Moncton to drop off his load.

The return trip was more exciting, as Dad picked up a crate of various shellfish headed for Ontario. My brothers and I played in the still-freezing trailer with dead lobsters and crabs like they were toys. Liam sat up front with Dad in my mother's absence. I'm pretty sure the two blubbered their way back home. We weren't allowed to talk about Mom after that.

Tongue made himself at home the second we entered our motel room. He stripped without a hint of shame and hopped into the shower. I assumed that the place was crawling with bed bugs, so I didn't bother getting under the covers. There was banging coming from the room beside us, and down the hall: the usual sounds of screwing and fighting, which had long since lost any distinction for me. I tried to stay focused, but the memory of my mother had weighed me down. It was then that I realized that I wanted to find her. That I'd always wanted to find her, and others too. But I'll get to that later.

Tongue appeared at the bathroom door. He was wearing a towel wrapped around his melon head and one wrapped around his waist. He was slathering himself up with some kind of salve.

"Well, aren't you precious?"

Tongue ignored me and continued to work the stuff all over his body. It reeked of ginger spice.

"What do you got there?"

"Ointment."

"Yeah, but where did you get it?"

"Compliments," he mumbled. He seemed a little irked that I was taking him away from his beautification ritual. Bending down to grease up his ankles and feet, the towel fell, and I got a good peek of his forest and tree. I saw it all as Tongue balanced a foot against the edge of the bed and continued to find new places to baste.

"Jesus!" I turned away. It was like staring at the sun. But I knew I'd have to get used to his naked flesh if he was coming on this crusade with me. "I'm going to get the ice cream," I told him.

It was a calm summer sunrise. I knew that most of the stuff would have melted along the way, but I still hoped to get a taste before sleep. When I made it to the limo, I spotted two men staggering away from the greasy spoon attached to the motel. They were both bearded, pot-bellied, and hunched, walking with knuckles dragging. There was no way of telling where their shoulders ended and their faces began. Neckless. Underneath their trucker hats advertising cheap beer: tufts of wild, mangy hair. Trolls. I wasn't certain if they were coming from dinner or breakfast in that wee hour. On instinct, I felt for Tongue's knife in my pocket, which I'd held onto since the graveyard beauty parlour. I opened up the trunk and grabbed the big pails of ice cream. Then one of the trolls called out to me.

"Hey there. Ah, hello. Excuse me."

I'd gut them both if they came too close, but when they did, something in their voices changed my mind.

"Pardon me, miss," said the shorter and heavier of the two. "I couldn't help noticing you're missing a muffler."

I reeled around. "That's right," I said, and slammed the trunk.

"Are you the one doing the driving or are you the one being drove?" he continued.

"What do you mean?"

"Limo. That's a fancy ride. I mean, are you being carted around or are you doing the carting?"

"Oh right. The car's mine."

"Decent," Troll One said.

They pressed their chubby faces against the tinted windows, and I could see that they were harmless. Just easily impressed by the appearance of wealth.

"Yeah, fancy," Troll Two, the one with bigger ears, said. "You don't think we could get a peek inside, do you? Never been in a limo before."

I put the ice cream pails on the ground. Just in case my instincts were failing me, I clutched the knife in my pocket while I opened the door. They piled inside.

"Right on! Ooh la la!" They were loving it: squishing their asses against the soft leather, scratching their beards and privates while their stubby legs were free to roam in the back seat. Then they pushed themselves out and were beside me on the earth again.

"Well, I think I can help you. See that sign over there?" Troll One pointed to the garage across the road.

"Jerry's Place. Yeah, I was gonna head over there in the morning," I told him.

"No need," he said. "I'm Jerry." He was so happy that he was Jerry. His entire cherubic body seemed to smile at me as a low, raspy laugh bubbled up from inside his round belly.

"Does she need a special size muffler?" I asked. "Any chance you might have one on hand?"

"Could do, could do...." Jerry was suddenly all business. "Fran, get down and have a peek. You're skinner than I am." He laughed.

"Yeah, but I'm drunker too, Jer." Fran was proud of his joke but went ahead and rolled himself under Henrietta. "Oh, yeah, nope, she'd be a special order."

I suddenly pictured myself stuck in that fleabag motel for a week with trolls crawling around on all fours looking for their keys and false teeth.

"Christ. How long?" I asked.

"Hard to say," Jerry piped in. "Depends."

"On what?" I asked.

"On how much you got." He rubbed his breakfast sausage fingers together, then sniffed them.

I was in no mood to barter, so I pulled out a bunch of hundreds. The two men went silent and began licking their lips. "I'll give you five now and another five if you can have me back on the road by tomorrow afternoon."

Jerry agreed and took the cash.

It was my first taste of instant control. I'd never considered the true power of money before. I'd always been on the other side, clamouring for it as Jerry and Fran were. They were desperate for it. Pathetic. "And there's a tip in it for you if you can get the dent out of the roof."

"That's just fine." Jerry was otherwise speechless.

I knew I had left myself vulnerable. That I'd shown them I had dough. That I'd paid for services I hadn't yet received. Christ, I couldn't even be sure that this troll was Jerry the mechanic. I suppose I wanted them to try to con me, rob me, or come after me. Just to have them try. The money had empowered me, as had the thought of getting the fuck out of Dodge.

Jerry got into the front and slipped Henrietta into neutral while Fran pushed from the back. They heaved the long white limousine into the parking lot across the street. I came back inside our room to find that Tongue had gone back into the shower. The water was going, and I was bugged because I didn't want him to use up all the hot.

"Hey," I said, knocking on the door, "you had your turn. I want mine."

But Tongue didn't answer.

"I brought in the ice cream." I figured I'd already met all his meat, so I pushed through and went inside the bathroom.

Tongue was in the shower, but it wasn't a stream of hot water he was under; it was a freezing cold mist coming off his skin into the air. Tongue was standing under the assault, trying not to move, making high-pitched sounds in his throat. His testicles had shrivelled and receded inside him, but they were still the size of pine cones. His body was a mess of pink hives.

"What the hell happened to you?"

Tongue pointed to the empty bottle of complimentary lotion that lay on the floor outside the tub. I assumed it must have been made from turpentine and Jerry's spunk, or else it was one hundred percent turpentine or one hundred percent troll spunk. Tongue's teeth were chattering in his head. Even his magical tongue had been attacked and seemed to swell, although it always seemed to swell.

"Rinse it off you," I told him.

"Burns," he whimpered.

"You shouldn't have used the whole bottle, damn it." But there was no point scolding him. The sprouting field of strawberries on his arms, chest, back, ass, legs, and ankles was punishment enough. "I'll see if I have anything in my bag."

In the other room, I realized that I'd left my bag in Henrietta. Not the money box, as I was guarding that with my life. But my Ziploc bag of goodies; it was still in the limo. I headed across to Jerry's, hoping not to find the trolls wanking in the back seat. I found the bag where I'd left it in the glove compartment and returned to the motel.

Tongue was no longer in pain. He'd poured both pails of melted ice cream into the tub and was writhing around in it, as happy as a pig in murky, thick, beige shit. The cool cream was soothing his rash, and he was getting a few licks too.

I woke up late the next afternoon and found Tongue asleep and stuck to the tub, snoring. I'd had a horrible time of it myself with the bed bugs and knew we'd be better off sleeping in the limo from then on. I stepped outside for my breakfast cigarette, and to my surprise, I found the two trolls towelling off Henrietta. She sparkled. Tongue's rooftop dent had been hammered out, and a new muffler was secured underneath. I paid them for their fine work.

"You boys work quick," I said.

"Got lucky," said Jerry. "We found a '77 hearse in the scrapyard over in Gananoque. Perfect match."

Fran and Jerry were beaming at their distorted reflections in the tinted windows. "Still curious who's getting the royal treatment," Fran said.

Tongue emerged from the motel like a Sasquatch: bewildered, nude, and covered in his mess.

"Go shower up," I told him. "And for Christ's sake, put some clothes on. We're hitting the road in ten."

Tongue walked back into the room sheepishly, wagging his sticky junk in the wind. Jerry and Fran regarded him with apt wonder.

10

The photograph of the infant in blue had proven to be more of a distraction to me hidden at the bottom of the cigar box like some dog's bone than out in the open staring back at me. Surely, my father had planned for it to stir up the whole mess inside me, and it had. I'd been thinking about it on long stretches of road, staring at headlights of transport trucks shining like relentless inquisitors' beams—taunting. For secrets, like regrets, like bruises under heavy makeup, like all shame, can never be truly buried. They grow underground. Roots spread unwieldy and gnarled and strangle, usually in the dead of night when you're alone with your breathing and blossoming sickness.

But it wasn't night now, and I wasn't alone, and as we crossed into Quebec, I let Tongue in on my buried treasure. He was stretched out in the back.

"You want to see something?"

"Yes."

"Pull back the floor mat."

Tongue searched around but couldn't find the place.

"Over to the right," I instructed. But he was lost, so I pulled over to the side of the road. We had veered off the main highway a few days earlier and were taking in farmland. We'd been staring at wheat and smelling cows for miles.

"Back here." I showed Tongue where the red floor mat lifted up. Underneath was a latch to a compartment that housed a tire iron and a jack. "I'm showing you this in case something bad happens to me," I told him. "But you have to keep it a secret."

Tongue didn't like the sound of it. I don't know how this bovine managed to gain my complete trust so quickly, or maybe I did. He was the only person I ever met who never once threatened me. I reached into the compartment and pulled out the cigar box. Tongue loved a good surprise. Really, the hidden compartment alone would have been enough for him. When I produced the box, his eyes widened, and he began to bare a wall of white teeth. But his big dumb expression changed the instant I pulled off the lid, revealing the money. Tongue turned away in a kind of disgusted vexation. I could see it made him nervous. I'd disappointed him somehow.

"What's up? It's clean," I told him. "I didn't steal it. I earned every last cent."

But Tongue refused to look.

"There's more," I told him.

"Naw, naw, naw." He was getting more anxious.

"Not money. Although I don't see the problem.

You gonna pay for gas? I wanted to show you this." I retrieved the photograph of my infant son and handed it to him.

Tongue held the picture in his hands as if it were made of delicate glass. As if he were holding the actual child in his big dumb grip and was careful not to drop him. His eyes went wide again, and I saw in them a slow steady burn of light. "Name?" he asked.

"I don't know," I told him. And I didn't. "Never named him. Never touched him. Never actually saw him except for that picture." Tongue hated my words. "That picture was taken the day he was born. He was cut out of me." I pulled up my shirt and showed Tongue the scar on my belly. He wanted to trace his finger along the mark, so I let him. "By the time I woke up from the C-section, they'd already taken him away." I pulled down my shirt and closed up the box of cash. I placed the box back inside the floor, latched up the compartment, and pulled the floor mat back into position. Tongue stared at the picture in his hands. I lit a cigarette. "Pretty fucked, eh?"

He was thinking on it. I could see that he wanted to ask me more, but he didn't. Instead, he opened up his mouth like a lion and lifted up his giant tongue. He then blurted out some incomprehensible slobber-blather: "Dey cuff me here coz it was attached."

I peered inside to find the remnants of the clipping. He'd been born tongue-tied.

"Born attached," he said.

Then I started pulling off the red boot on my left foot, the cigarette dangling from my lips. "Oh yeah? Well, lookie here." My sock off, I held the back of my leg and shoved my foot into his face. "You see that black spot?" Tongue inspected. "That's a roofer's nail. That nail's been in my foot for twenty years." Tongue poked at the metal in my freak foot.

I had stepped on the thing during my seventh birthday party. My father and some of his incompetent friends were tarring the roof of our house, nailing shingles they'd most likely pinched from a shipment. Unckey Dirk was there too, probably fetching pails of hot tar. Four drunk idiots roofing is a recipe for disaster, and I'm pretty sure Dirk fell off twice. I know he got himself stuck in the chimney, or maybe that was on a different occasion—I can't be certain. I had a friend over for my birthday, the Little Amanda. She was this scrawny, anemic thing who lived next door. Rumour had it that she was one of Dad's illegitimates. She had a compulsion for pulling her pants down to pee in front of boys. My brothers knew this well and were eager to join in the squatfest.

As the hack construction crew worked above us with nail guns, my brothers and I, along with the Little Amanda, goofed around in the backyard. We played spitting tag. The person who is it, or "spit," has to try to spit on the other players in order to build a team of spitters. If you get hit with spit, you join in the chase until it's a gang of spitters chasing after one player.

I was quick that day, unfortunately, the last one standing. This meant that I was forced to outrun the wads of the whole pack. I remember being at the far side of the yard. I could see the silhouettes of the ass clowns on the roof against the backdrop of the piercing sun. The Little Amanda and my brothers were making a plan near the barbeque pit—plotting on how to rain down on me.

Then a scuffle broke out on the roof. Maybe this is when Dirk took his tumble. My father was screaming at a guy named Lance. He had him by the collar and was making to toss him over the edge. The maniacs all started laughing and shooting their nail guns into the air; they were having a gay old time.

With my attention on the men, I hadn't noticed that my brother Randy and the Little Amanda had come creeping up from the far side of me. I was surrounded. They started spitting. I bolted straight ahead, but the pack moved in. They were yelling like the roofers. That's when I felt the pierce of the nail go in. I dropped down to the grass and instantly howled, bawling my eyes out. The team stayed on task and drenched me even with the thing stuck quivering in my foot. Later on, the doctor wasn't able to remove it entirely.

Tongue squeezed the skin around the metal.

"I don't feel a thing. Doesn't hurt. Good luck charm."

After marvelling at it for a few moments, Tongue very nonchalantly began to undo his belt and slide off his great big pants.

"Whoa, whoa, whoa. What exactly am I looking at?" I asked.

Tongue contorted his massive leg up and over his massive head like an acrobat doing a fancy floor routine. Once again, I saw that he was indeed all rubber.

"Here!" Tongue struggled to remain upright. Puffing hard, he had one hand under his quivering shank and the other still clutching the picture of my kid. "Here! Here!" He was sputtering, on the verge of blowing a gasket. "Birthmark."

"I see it. Jesus! What is it?"

The mark was a purple splat with blue around the edges. It looked like a land formation on a map. At the same time, it resembled a kind of deformed bird. In its own sick way, it was beautiful. There seemed to be precision to it, a kind of logic to the design. I felt as though I were staring at a cloud that the viewer transforms in the mind's eye to whatever they want it to be. Or some abstract painting, the work of some mad visionary. Sitting in that smoke-filled limousine with the half-naked 250-pound contortionist, I saw Tongue's birth splotch turn into the image of a parachuting turkey on fire, then into the Galápagos Islands, before settling as the profile of a Greek god with a beard of bees—a stinging Zeus or Apollo.

"Impressive."

He agreed and started to pull himself back together again.

I showed Tongue all the cigarette burns on my

wrists. He said they looked like ladybugs crawling. I showed him the trick with my thumb; missing a joint, it can bend back to my forearm. For his part, Tongue revealed a third nipple on his chest and a mole on his shoulder that was so goddamn big that it had a mole of its own growing on top of it. I don't know how I'd missed them before, not that I was looking that closely.

But Tongue's belly button was the most magical of all our mutations. He lifted up his shirt and asked me for my cigarette lighter. "Give it."

"Don't set yourself on fire."

He dismissed my remarks and proceeded to insert the entire lighter inside the gaping hole at the centre of his belly. It vanished inside his second mouth.

"Some trick."

He pulled it out with a pop and handed it to me.

"No, keep it."

"Deep, huh?"

"Yup." I wondered what else he could hide up there. I knew where I'd be hiding my stash if we ever got pulled over. I knew that Tongue's belly could conceal all that I wanted.

As we were getting ready to move on, Tongue rummaged around his duffle and pulled out a silver necklace. He poked a hole in the photograph of my kid, fed the necklace through it, and hung it on the rear-view mirror. I started up the car. Tongue picked at his navel.

11

We found a country market a few towns over. It was an overbuilt wooden structure, painted up in a cheery cherry red and white. *Chez Bonne Maman.* The place was attached to a rolling farm that was open to the public. A perfect outing for Tongue. It was summertime, and the kiddies were out in full force, swarming the grounds. A real francophonic hullabaloo. Despite the stench of hot manure outside, the feel inside the dining area when we entered was real rustic magic. Tongue was all saliva, sniffing after the homemade cuisine. I admit that I too felt weak breathing in the sweetness of freshly baked bread.

Bonne Maman was behind the counter, tending to the wants of a family who seemed to want one of everything on the menu. She was serving up custard, pastries, coffee, milkshakes, and a variety of things with jam. Man, everything looked so good. There was a purity to the place that was so foreign to me that my stomach cried. Tongue was silent and still like a predator in the wild. He was hunting out the sweetness of life, sniffing the air, licking his lips. We were next in line, but I thought he might clear away the children in front of us with one swooping movement of his arm, jump the counter, and start feasting on Bonne Maman herself. Fill his belly button with grape jelly.

"Know what you want?"

"Do."

Tongue was no nonsense. Very serious. I realized then that we'd been eating only various forms of gut rot since setting out. There's only so much beef jerky and pork rinds one can take. We'd been eating fast food and candy bars ever since our escape, and only now in the presence of all that warmth did I realize my insides had turned to acid.

"*Bienvenue. Qu'est-ce que tu veux?*"

Maman had called us over to her in French. It took me a second to realize this, but Tongue knew what was going on, and he bounded towards the counter.

The only words I know in French are *bonjour* and *merde*: "good day" and "shit." I also know the word for "tired"—*fatigué*—because it sounds like "fat" and "gay." We used to call a kid in school *fatigué* because he went around hollow-eyed in a kind of trance. He was also fat and gay, and this pleased our mature playground sensibility greatly.

I began to stammer out an order in English: "Uh, bacon and eggs. Coffee—ah *merde*, I mean *café*."

I also know the word for "coffee." That's an easy one. But before I could finish, Tongue moved in front of me in a condescending sidestep. Keep in mind the blob had only ever really grunted at me for the entire time I knew him. He'd sometimes string full sentences together, but I was never really clear as to what he was actually saying. In front of Maman, however, in that dairy farm wonderland, my slobbering travelling companion sang out the most eloquent, most resonant, most beautiful French I'd ever heard.

"*Bonjour, ma chère Maman. Ça va?*"

Maman beamed up at his grinning face.

"*Je m'excuse,*" Tongue continued, "*mais mon amie ne parle pas le français. Tout est très bon. Que recommandez-vous ce matin?*"

I was floored by his elocution. How he kept his tongue from getting in the way of all of those rolling sounds, I couldn't understand. It was as if there were some poet from Montreal inside his mouth. He was still the hulking boob I'd come to know, but as he spoke French, I began to see him differently. Maman, who was quite taken with my big French-speaking giant, began to list off the entire menu in so fast a ramble that I couldn't imagine she was actually saying words. Sounded like a bush full of birds to me. To each item described to him, Tongue responded accordingly.

"*Très bien.*"

"*Délicieux.*"

"*Mon Dieu, ça c'est robuste.*"

This went on for about five minutes. Then he finally ordered: "*Un croque-monsieur pour moi et des œufs et jambon pour Winnie. Aussi, une tasse de café et une grande tasse de café au lait, s'il vous plaît, Maman."*

Maman sprang into action and called out the order to the kitchen in back.

"*Vingt dollar cinquante,*" she said to Tongue, who turned to me and held out his meat mitt in this dainty way that I'd never seen before. I pulled out some dough and handed it to him. He was a big tipper.

We took a seat by a huge bay window overlooking the farm. It was as though I'd stepped into another world, and I had. In that moment, I too thought I could speak another language and beautifully. I longed to. The main barn on the property was buzzing with visitors who were having a look at the animals. A horse-drawn carriage was giving rides. Everyone was eating in that paradise, and I even started to enjoy the stink of cow *merde.*

"I didn't know you could speak French."

"Yup. *Oui.*" Tongue was back to his monosyllabic grunting.

"You speak it so well."

"Uh-huh."

Our food arrived then, and it completed the country scene. Big portions of it too. We feasted. I didn't care that Tongue's croque-monsieur (his ham, eggs, and toast) was running down his face like mucus. When we'd finished, I asked if he wanted to take a look around. He did.

Despite the sound of children's voices surrounding

us, and those hissing inside my head, the country brought a quiet with it that seemed to untangle knots in my shoulders and neck. I moved differently through those grounds. Tongue, too, content with a real meal, had a slightly different gait. He'd passed on the horse-drawn carriage ride and preferred instead to look at the cows. In one of the many outbuildings in the complex, Bonne Papa was giving a milking lesson, working on one of the massive creatures. There was a small circle of well-behaved and attentive children sitting close by on haystacks, arranged like a barnyard classroom. Papa was an elderly, rustic gentleman, who, with great care, was showing how to grip and angle the beast's teat. He pulled, and out shot rapid sprays of pure white.

Tongue was completely engrossed in this lesson, pure in his wonder, but I wasn't. It always happens to me. Other people's amusement usually pisses me off. Papa allowed the kids to take a squeeze, and their excitement mixed with fear returned me to my caustic self. I hung back near a clucking chicken coop as Tongue joined the others. He was overexcited, which wasn't anything new, but Papa cautioned him before he allowed him to take his turn milking the animal. Once again, Tongue was all French poetry in his actions. The liquid repulsed me and made me gag. The very idea that I'd ever once drunk the contents of a cow's udders horrified me, and I vowed I'd never do it again. Tongue's pail filled up in that shitty barn, and I started thinking about all the creatures that had been slaughtered in the very place where I was standing. I wondered what they would do to old Bessie when she was all dried out. When they'd drained her of every last drop. Would they cut her from end to end? Would they rip her open or put her down with a single bullet before grinding her down into burger? That's the way my mind has always worked. I enter calm waters with caution, never quite trusting they'll soothe, and even if I do start to feel a trickle of cooling, fresh pleasure, it isn't long before I'm consumed and fighting not to drown.

I was thinking this way as Tongue made the children laugh with his stupid squeezing grimaces, sticking out his massive tongue and biting it. Pink and naked. Over in the corner, a man was hammering a horseshoe onto a monstrous Clydesdale. The clinking of the hammer against hoof was a kind of tyrannical metronome, and I knew I needed out.

A young farmhand rushed past me then and went to speak to Bonne Papa, who ended the milking party abruptly. The two of them exited the barn with Tongue in hot pursuit. I moved away from the group. The sun was beating down, and I followed an endless fence that stretched the length of the property and beyond until I found a secluded spot under a patch of trees.

I popped a few pills and lit a cigarette, and in a few minutes I was able to breathe. And because I was outside and alone, and because nature was bearing down on me in that open field where everyone else was free to frolic in a language I didn't speak, I gave myself permission and squatted over a pleasant pile of hay, pulled down my panties, and peed there. Right there like an animal or the Little Amanda. I stood up to discover the liquid pooling and reflecting the sun's glare. I finished my cigarette, watching the urine trickle away and seep into the earth. Then I kicked at some loose gravel surrounding me and buried my mess.

I headed back to the barns to find Tongue shoulder-deep inside a cow's seeping backside. His eyes bulged, and there seemed to be blue smoke coming out of his huge nostrils. Bonne Papa was slipping him hushed French orders. And I watched in horror as the man with the huge tongue trembled, on the verge of eruption, as he slid out a wet, blind, and braying newborn calf from its mother.

12

We had a close call on the road the night after I ran out of pills. I don't think I was speeding. Either way, I was messed up, and I had to swerve to avoid an oncoming transport truck. It was enough for me to know that I needed a break from driving. I'd been doing all the driving all the way from Ontario, and riding cold turkey now I was a wreck. We'd take pit stops whenever Tongue got hungry, and I'd try to stretch as much as I could, but I was burning out fast behind the wheel. Tongue suggested we watch the stars since I'd almost killed us, so we stretched out on top of the roof of the limo, and my bones popped and crackled like fireworks.

The sky was a deep pink, and the sun still lingered, stubborn, as if it had some unfinished plans for the day. The moon traced the far-off outline of the horizon—a simple chalk impression. We lay on our backs, and I felt heavy despite the vastness surrounding us. Even though all we watched was sky, I knew we were desperately attached to the earth.

I was practicing my deep breathing, something Tongue always seemed to do. He sucked back the air in such a purposeful and belaboured way that I thought there'd be none left for the rest of us wretches. The relaxation exercise wasn't working. I'd run out of pills down around Trois-Rivières. I couldn't sleep anymore, especially listening to Tongue snore inside of Henrietta. I'd been upping my dose to drown him out and figured that that's how I'd run out so fast. Fighting withdrawal now.

I'd managed to get clean many times throughout my life, and I knew how to do it, usually by replacing the fix with a bottle. But being on the road had presented a greater challenge. I tried to explain it to Tongue, and he just looked at me and told me to breathe the way I was doing now on that roof under that suffocating sky. I wanted to be turned off. Sleep it off. Every inch of me was crawling, and I wanted to be unconscious to stop the constant movement of insects under my skin.

"This is bullshit. We're gonna have to find something. I'm starting to lose it." I felt as if I were underwater. Tongue was used to my outbursts and said nothing. He was conversing with the moon, which I saw as another cruel bitch. How many times had I called the moon a bitch? "I'm so fucked. Can't sleep. Can't stay awake. You want us to crash?" My brain was turning into mush.

Then I had a fit. I actually started kicking my feet

hard against the roof of Henrietta. I wanted to smash something, anything. This went on for a few minutes, banging and gnashing teeth, until I started to cry. Tongue reached over and held me. I tried to surrender to him and bury my face in his shoulder. I tried to ride this wave out, and it was real comfort, until a flash of panic burst up stemming from my knees, and I lashed out at him, biting into his enormous bicep. He didn't make a sound. He pulled away from me and almost fell off the roof of the limo, and I started to laugh cruelly. He sat up, rubbing his arm. He was seething and pink, and I was glad.

"Why do I have to drive you around, anyway? I'm not your goddamn chauffeur. What makes you so goddamn special?" My words seemed to colour the sky, for now it was black, all black except for the moon. Despite my mania, it was a legitimate question. I had never considered the possibility of Tongue taking over at the wheel. "Can't you drive, Tongue?" He glared at me then. I'd never called him that out loud before. "What's the matter? Cat's got your tongue, Tongue? I asked you a fucking question." I kicked my feet hard against the hood.

I suppose I was chasing any feeling I could get as long as it was different from how I felt at that moment. Seeing Tongue's neck go pink and his ears burn bright was the closest thing to it. Feel as I feel as I'm feeling it.

"Maybe you could pull us like an ox. I can tie a fucking rope around your neck, and you can pull us, because I'm not driving another mile until I get a hit." My howling rang out across the neighbouring fields.

I think I remember screaming something else. Out of nowhere, Tongue sprang to his feet. He'd had enough of my hateful words. In one motion, he stood on top of the limo, grabbed hold of my ankles, and pulled me straight up into the air. I dangled there. I cleared the top of the limo by a good three feet. He had me suspended like some frantic rag doll. All the crap in my pockets—lighters, change, lipstick—it all fell out and dinged off the roof. My shirt rose so that my bra was exposed, and my hair was an upside-down mess. I fought like an animal.

"Put me down, you freak!" I was furious, but terrified too. I wondered if he planned on twirling me around like that before sending me flying. I'd end up in some cornfield with a broken neck. "Put me down, Jesus!" I was a wreck.

I could feel the blood rushing to my head as he refused to let go of my ankles. Tongue held me stiff. He didn't react to my words or flailing fists. I was nothing in his grip. I felt as though I was about to pop. I don't remember when I finally stopped struggling, but it really wasn't too long before I blacked out.

Still, seconds before crossing into the delirium, as it became harder and harder to scream and curse, as though the electric charge within my body began to flicker like a faulty circuit, I thought of my mother once again. Really, it was just the image of her swinging body on the day she tried to hang herself in the basement.

From early days, I knew of an iron rod that ran the length of the ceiling, where Mom used to hang up laundry to dry. This was before we started washing our own clothes. We hated going down there because, besides the usual smell of turpentine and mold, all those clothes hanging from the ceiling seemed to come to life in the shadows. It was as if a whole other family was down there suspended in midair in the room. Dad's coveralls; a few of Mom's nightgowns; and, of course, a parade of boy's trousers, all of them different sizes with knees ripped; worn-out tee shirts; a few of my skirts. All that wet material hanging, just hanging. Lumped, soaked through, dripping onto a stone-cold floor. She'd often forget to go down and pick it up after it was dry, so the whole room was haunted by these phantoms of ourselves. A ray of light would shoot through the one storm window, and it only made the ghosts seem all the more disturbed. We were terrified to go down there when this city of disembodied parts was out, and sometimes we'd dare each other to, or else somebody would shove someone down to contend with the basement dwellers and the rats.

So that's why when my brother Randy came running, screaming that Mom was hanging from that black rod in the basement, we didn't believe him. We all assumed that he'd just envisioned her joining the usual group of hanging clothes. But he swore up and down. My oldest brother, Liam, seemed to take the vision more seriously. He went down to investigate. He's the one who cut her down. She survived it shut up in her room for the next week, and it wasn't long before we took her to New Brunswick to get locked up. To dry out on somebody else's line in the Maritimes.

I must have slept for fourteen hours. I awoke stuffed inside a pair of Tongue's massive pants and his big green sweater with a hood, which was pulled up around my head and tied tightly together. I lay in the back of the limo, bundled. The smell surrounding me was intense lilac. I freed myself from his makeshift cocoon to discover lilacs sprouting inside Henrietta. They were everywhere. As if I'd been buried under the flowers. Tongue wasn't with me inside the limo, and as I stepped out into the sunlight, I panicked because he wasn't outside either. I wondered if he'd set off on his own journey without me. If there was a lost child and a mother of his own whom he had to find. I wondered if he'd ever been there at all. Ever existed. There was no trace of him.

My head was split in two by an axe—right down the centre. It was another stage of getting clean, but I was grateful for the sleep. Tongue hadn't left a note, not that I thought he could write. Just the flowers. And upon searching the front seat, I found that he'd left me some fruit too. A basket of strange-looking berries. They may have been mulberries or boysenberries—I don't know. They were deep red and engorged. I needed something, so I decided to take the risk that they weren't poisonous and started to stuff them into my dry, cracked mouth. They exploded. Lit me up. I wiped the juice off my lips with my sleeves.

Sitting on the hood, contemplating the berries and the pain in my stomach, I watched as an antique pickup truck belched up beside me on the road. A farmer was carrying a pack of clucking chickens in his bed. He slowed down beside the limo, craned his neck out, stared at me with bug eyes, and then continued on his way. That's when I heard the singing in the fields. It wasn't the wind in the reeds because there was no wind, and there were no reeds either. I traced the landscape with blurred vision, trying to locate the source, and I found it. The song rose and echoed throughout the fields around me. It was Tongue. He was real. He was singing opera. A rich tenor, carrying full notes to a herd of grazing horses. He was wearing my father's chauffeur's hat, his pant legs rolled up to his knees, carrying a huge bushel of lilacs. For their part, the horses seemed pleased enough to continue to graze for the duration of the serenade, which seemed to rise in never-ending vibrato until it was done. Then Tongue turned and headed towards me on the road with a goofy, contented look on his face.

"Bravo," I said when he'd arrived.

Sweat glistened off him, ran in streaks down his cheeks. Tongue dumped more flowers into the back of the limo. "Did ya breathe?"

I suddenly understood the mad logic in his remedy, for he had knocked me out without leaving any marks.

Held me upside down until the mad blood rushed to my dead head. He'd replaced the smell of rot with lilacs and kept watch over me like a cowherd over a mad cow on Benzedrine.

"How long I been out?"

"Days."

He went at the berries in the basket, and I wondered whose fields he'd been pillaging but knew in that moment that all the land belonged to Tongue.

"We better get a move on. You must be starving."

Under the gushing red juice, he flashed me a mischievous smile. I wondered if he'd been eating the livestock too. He went around to the trunk, and I followed. Opening it up, he revealed a collection of pies and some empty dishes. "Found 'em cooling in da windows. Finders keepers."

Tongue had managed to keep us both alive for another couple of nights, and I suppose I was glad for it. The sun was once again overhead, and the earth was charged with life. A sweat broke on my forehead, and I was happy for that too. I knew the toxins needed to seep out of my broken body.

"Let's hit the road. I need to shower."

"Nope." Tongue snapped to, and he held out the hawk keychain. "Me." He then plopped himself down behind the wheel.

13

I spent the next week trying to get clean while teaching Tongue how to drive—a brutal combo. I'd never taught anybody anything before, and I was as bad a teacher as he was a driver. The worst of the withdrawals didn't help matters. Tongue's biggest problem was that he liked turning the wheel too much. I mean, even going straight he was always wanting to spin, ride around zigzag. Besides that, his huge size-thirteen boots were heavy. Lead feet led to instant acceleration or hard stops. He was bouncing me around in the back. I was at the mercy of a tyrannical Tilt-A-Whirl operator. It made my already furious nausea worse. When I shouted instructions to him, he would let go of the wheel and take his foot off the gas, or he'd brake until I was done before following the order. All the while making sounds in his throat, mimicking the roar of the engine or the screech of the tires. He was fearless too. We'd knocked over a dozen wooden mailboxes, ended up in a lettuce patch, and somehow managed to get the rear axle entangled in a thicket of pussy willows.

I'd lost all sense of direction and time. Tongue had taken so many turns that I was half expecting to come to the edge of the earth at any moment. Surely we were no longer heading east to New Brunswick. It didn't matter to me, really. I couldn't be sure that my mother was even alive, and if she were, whether she was still rotting in the hospital where we'd left her all those years ago—if the hospital was even still standing. I figured that Tongue's ambling was as reliable as any map of a directionless, futureless future. Man, I was feeling sorry for myself.

I do have to give the galoot credit though. Not once did he lose his cool. Not once did he shout back at me or break down. And at times I was really giving it to him. My words of discouragement felt like poisoned darts shooting out of my mouth. Bullets or big sleek bugs coughed up and fired out, sent buzzing around his big head. But they would not penetrate. In my quieter moments, when we'd pull over for the night, I was ashamed of my words and their splinter spikes. I heard my father's tone in them, that gravelly sarcasm, stones in the throat, questions intended to break Tongue down:

"Is that left or right?"

"Do you know the difference between shoulder and road?"

"Do you think swamps are meant to be driven in?"

"Do you see the road?"

"Are you truly retarded?"

"Do you think we're flying?"

"You want to fucking die?"

I hated myself for carrying on this way. For gnawing away at the man who was clearly doing his best. For chewing on his spirit and spitting it out the window. But no matter how many times I promised myself I would lay off, the very next time he'd get us stuck in the mud or I'd catch him staring at a weathervane instead of the road, I'd jump on him and stick pins in the back of his bull neck.

"You can't drive on the other side of the road just because it has a better view of the silo and the pigs!"

But just as I was ready to give up on him, Tongue turned it around. Literally. He turned old Henrietta around in a magical maneuver to avoid a head-on collision with a drunk driver. The asshole was riding erratic in a sputtering red sedan. It was getting dark, raining too, and we were planning on turning in for the night when this son of a bitch with only one working headlight appeared in a wet flash in front of us. I saw it in slow motion and could barely bark out the warning when Tongue jerked the wheel to the side to avoid the crash and jerked it straight again to avoid a tree.

We came to a sudden stop. I was frantic. Never wearing a seatbelt, I'd ended up in the front with Tongue. He remained still, white-knuckled, clutching the wheel. Then he let out a bellow that rattled the world: "Aaaaaaaaaaaaaaaaaaah!"

"That shit-ass!" I was glad to have a new target for my verbal shooting practice. I looked back to see that the prick had ended up in a ditch. I bounded out of the car and descended on him. The red car was also missing both taillights, and the right window had been patched with a garbage bag and electrical tape. The asshole was fiddling with the door. I banged on the hood.

"What the hell, man!" I was screaming, and it felt great. I persevered despite the storm outside. "That could have been my life!"

The driver was a bloated pig of a man. His swine eyes bulged when he saw me at the window. When I opened the door, I saw that he wasn't wearing any shoes or socks or pants, just a tight white tee shirt with mustard and puke stains and a pair of boxer shorts with the Canadian maple leaf and piss stains on them. A flask lay next to him on the passenger seat. He was mumbling something about the rain. I admit that I wanted to kill him, or, at least, I wished him dead.

"What were you thinking, you drunk fuck?"

He stepped out of his car in his bare feet and staggered about. The piglet showed a pathetic erection poking out of his shorts. I could see that the near crash had excited him. When he managed to stand upright, he started staring at my chest. My wet shirt revealed the outline of my bra, though the pig's tits were bigger than mine.

"Fuck you," he muttered.

I slapped him across his peameal bacon face, and he laughed. Then he pushed me, and I fell to the ground. Now, I didn't want Tongue to intervene. I wanted to stick my knife in this guy's gut—slaughter him. I pulled out my weapon, but by the time I got to my feet, Tongue, still charged up from his stunt-driving brilliance, rushed at the drunk bastard and sent him running up the road. His chubby trotters trudged over the wet stones.

"I'm fine," I told him. Tongue saw his Swiss Army tool in my hands. "Gonna slash his tires so he can't drive again tonight and kill somebody."

"Yeah!" Tongue really liked that idea very much.

As I went around to puncture the back tire, Tongue reached into the front seat, grabbed hold of the steering wheel with both hands, and ripped the thing off. He hurled it like a discus into the neighbouring field. He did the same with the side mirrors. Pulled them off like they were nothing. Tongue head-butted the windshield, and the sound of breaking glass was beautiful. Then he pulled off all four doors and left them lying on the side of the road. When he was through dismantling the car, he was out of breath and grinning.

Before we left, I reached inside and grabbed the flask. Or maybe I grabbed the flask first and then saw Tongue pull off the doors—I can't be certain. Either way, I knew that the incident meant that Tongue had graduated from my driver's ed and that I didn't have to keep constant watch over him.

After drying off in the back of Henrietta, Tongue resumed his rightful place in the driver's seat, and I got wasted drinking from that asshole's flask and welcomed sleep.

14

I awoke to the sounds of a goddamn jamboree. I had slept well, stretched out in the rear of the limo, but a motley mix of singing wanderers had invaded my private chambers. Tongue, left to his own devices while I slept, had stopped to pick up every hitchhiker thumbing their way to the east coast.

"Morning," said a man sitting across from me. He wore loose khakis and a red plaid shirt. His grin showed a few missing teeth. He carried a green rucksack on his lap. His face was badly scarred from a mess of acne.

I didn't respond. I was completely bewildered, waking up to a bad dream in the key of G.

"You been asleep for ages." The woman next to him who'd been doing the most of the singing stopped and said this to me. She had a slight pink sunburn on her round cheeks, and her straw-blonde hair poked out under a colourful bandana. She was breastfeeding a child under an unbuttoned jean shirt. The kid was staring at me, stuck to his mother.

"Big Ben was kind enough to stop for us a few towns back. You headed to the festival in Moncton too?"

"Big Ben?" I asked.

The toothless guy pointed to Tongue up front.

"Great guy." This came from a man who was squeezed left of the breastfeeding woman. He was round, bald, bearded, and burned, eating a chicken wing, wearing big mailman shorts. His socks were pulled up to his knobby knees. Squeezed in beside him was another guy whose chin was attached to his throat. He had a poorly grown goatee that must have been in place to distinguish the two. He had hollow rat eyes and a long nose. The ugger didn't speak but nodded furiously. As he did, he revealed an Adam's apple the size of a fist.

"Where'd he pick you up?" the chicken man asked me.

I was trying to wrap my head around the invasion, also trying not to lose my cool. I didn't respond.

"I'm Hubert," said the guy in the khakis. "This is Bernice, my beloved." He pointed to the lady with her tit out.

"Hi there," she said.

"Little fella's named Gorgy. He's my son." Bert beamed at his beloved and pulled back her shirt and kissed the baby's head.

"I'm Wayne Howl," the bald chicken man piped in with a mouthful of meat.

"And you?" I asked the guy with the Adam's apple.

"We don't know," Wayne Howl chimed in. "He

been riding with us all morn, but still hasn't said boo nor baa."

Adam's Apple nodded to confirm what Wayne Howl was saying about him.

"He's kinda shy," Howl continued. "Ain't ya?" He yelled this at Adam's Apple between chews.

Adam's Apple blushed and continued to nod. Bernice unhitched Gorgy from her teat. The kid hiccupped and burped, then glommed onto his mother's other nipple. I saw Howl sneak a peak at this. I wanted to throttle Tongue.

"Most folk these days won't stop for you if you gots a thumb out. Who woulda guessed we'd be getting a ride first class like this? Ooh la la, so fancy!"

They all agreed with this. Adam's Apple was bobbing up and down furiously.

"You want some chicken?" Howl asked, and he produced a grease-stained bucket from somewhere and held it out to me.

"No," I said.

"Suit yourself. Bertie? Bernice?"

The couple didn't want any either. Offering a drumstick to Adam's Apple, Howl raised his voice as if talking to a deaf person. *"You want a leg?!"*

Adam's Apple didn't respond, just plunged right into the bucket and pulled out a brown piece of wet bird and started chomping on it. Then Howl went at a new bone of his own. The entire time, Tongue refused to show his face. He had pushed up the tinted window that divided the back and the front seat; I stared daggers into it, hoping to catch his wandering eyes.

Bert and Bernice resumed singing the folk song that had woken me up. It was about the sinking of a ship on Lake Superior. Howl hummed along under big smacks of his chicken lips. Adam's Apple didn't do shit all but eat his chicken.

I'd hitchhiked once or twice when I was a kid. I took off from home those first few times, but I didn't get very far. It was before I had given up on ever finding my son. I remember once being picked up at a gas station by a Mountie who had spotted me sleeping at a bus stop. These hitchhikers were pleasant enough, and certainly not on the run from ghouls and dead maniacs, but it wasn't Tongue's place to decide who rode with us. By the time Gorgy started screaming, I'd had it. The kid's parents kept on singing, hoping to lull him to sleep.

"Whatsa matter? Whatsa matter?" Howl was making faces at the kid. He was smeared with grease now, and his nursery games only served to make Gorgy wail even louder, and still Burt and Bernice wouldn't change their goddamn tune.

"Who's got yer nose? Who's got yer nose?" Howl was loving every minute of it, but Gorgy wasn't. Gorgy hated that pudgy son of a bitch, and I did too.

Adam's Apple was terrorized, and he covered his ears with his bony hands, shut his shitty eyes, and started rocking back and forth. That's when I spotted the tire iron and jack lying on the floor. Someone had been messing with my cigar box of cash. I immediately went down on all fours and starting digging up the carpet to check on my hidden compartment.

"Move!" I shouted. Adam's Apple's feet were in my way. My head was right at the level of Wayne Howl's crotch, and he started shifting uneasy in his seat.

"Whatcha looking for down there, lady?" Howl's voice was shaky and froglike from swallowing bird.

I didn't respond, just continued to fuss with the latch until I had it open. The blood ran from my body. The cigar box with the money was gone.

"Billy!" I screamed. Gorgy screamed. Adam's apple screamed.

"Who's Billy?" Burt blurted out.

I started smacking on the back of Tongue's seat. "Oh, Billy? Stop this fucking car!"

"Please, dear." Bernice was bouncing Gorgy on her knee now, trying to get the kid to shut his trap.

"His name's Ben, darling." Wayne Howl pointed to the lettering on the tinted back window. "Ben."

They didn't know what to make of my outburst as I started to search under the seats by their feet. They began talking as if I weren't there.

"Not sure what's gotten into her," Burt said. "She's looking for something."

"Seems mad," Wayne Howl observed. Adam's Apple agreed.

"Did ya lose your contact lens, dear? Do you want

us to help you find it?" Wayne Howl asked me. Then he said to Burt, "She's certainly miffed about something. She's burrowing down there like a half-crazed weasel."

And I was. I was ready to turn the whole limousine inside out. I was ready to turn them inside out too. I'd start with Howl. Tear him a new asshole. Maybe he'd hidden the money at the bottom of his bucket of chicken.

After a few minutes of frantic searching, I demanded that Tongue stop the car. Well, I started cursing louder than Gorgy was crying, and Burt got Tongue to pull over.

"Ah, hey, Ben?" he called to Tongue. "I think you might want to make a pit stop. One of your passengers is none too pleased. We think she's lost her cell phone."

"Or her mind," Bernice muttered.

"Crikey," Wayne Howl added.

Adam's Apple stared at my grinding teeth.

Tongue came to a stop near a field that had a bunch of electrical towers. They looked like blown-out buildings. At the far side of the field was an enormous complex with smokestacks. It reminded me of the shitty factory land back home. The panic seized me then. We'd been driving for weeks, and I contemplated the horror of Tongue's having driven us all the way back to where we'd started. Or maybe it was just this sick feeling I had, wanting to locate the missing cash.

I burst out of the car, holding the tire iron, and I went around to the driver's side. It was locked. I started tapping hard on the window.

"Billy. Come on, Billy. We need to talk."

Tongue was hiding, but then very slowly he brought down the tinted window so that just the top of his ill-fitting chauffeur's hat was visible.

"Hey, you. Get out of there." I reached in and grabbed my father's hat so that the hole in Tongue's head could breathe. "Come on."

Tongue lowered the window another inch. He was scared, but, hell, so was I. I wondered if he'd lost the money or if it'd been taken by one of the hitchhikers, or if Tongue got hungry and ate it. Still, I was getting nowhere, so I changed my tune.

"I'm not mad," I tried to say coolly. "I just want to chat in private. I think you owe me an explanation. Don't you?"

But the big man refused to lower the window.

I've never had patience, and I certainly wasn't about to invest in it, so I reached in the crack of the window and tried grabbing at the idiot's ear. "Get the fuck out of there."

"Leave him be," Wayne Howl said. "Hey, Ben, why don't you just leave her?"

"Yeeeah...leave her be," Burt joined in. "We searched —there's no sunglasses back here."

"Stay out of it," I yelled back at the squatters. But I suddenly felt vulnerable. I'd been dispossessed. Why shouldn't Tongue just leave me there? They all seemed as though they knew exactly where they were headed, but I didn't.

I took notice of a pack of children playing in the field lined with electrical towers. Their far-off laughter broke me down even further. Then, to my surprise, the front passenger door opened, and out stepped yet another hitchhiker I hadn't noticed before. He wore brown soft leather cowboy boots and tight blue jeans. His western denim shirt was unbuttoned to the chest with the sleeves rolled to the elbows. He was terribly attractive: square shoulders and jaw, big blue eyes that could penetrate. That kind of perfect face that you want to either love or smash. Maybe with a tire iron. He had the longest hair I'd ever seen on a man. It was luscious: wavy and golden. He spoke in a deep, soothing voice that kind of went up at the end.

"Beautiful out, eh?" As he approached, I heard the crush of stones under his boot heels. "Look at those kids down there. They know it. It's a shame to see all of those ugly towers corrupting such a pretty scene. That old concrete monster, pumping out fumes into God's green grandeur. But those kids keep it charged."

I didn't know what the hell he was on about. Figured he was the one they sent to talk the crazy down off the roof.

"Who are you?" I asked.

"The eternal question. The only question, really. Who am I?" He laughed at his hack philosophy. "You want a name? Well, I'm Jack. You can call me that if you'd like, Winnie." Tongue must have filled him in. "You can call me anything you'd like."

"How about asshole?" I said.

Jack laughed. I hated his laugh. High-pitched and goofy, and he snorted too. "Yeah, you can call me that."

"Jackass?"

"Good. Good, I like that. A name I can easily live up to. Low expectations."

Jackass was all charm, and he knew it. He was that rare breed who could slow the world down to a pace that matched his own, singsong and smooth. I took him as a misplaced hippy. A con man complete with the false adornment of that incredible head of hair.

"Where'd he pick you up?" I asked. "Haight-Ashbury?"

"Be sure to wear flowers in your hair." Jackass laughed. "Don't be mad at the big fella," he said, avoiding the question. "That man in there—Constantine—he's all heart." If Jack had charmed Tongue, then Tongue had certainly charmed Jack. "Why don't you let me try to get him out for you? He's a gentle soul, you know. You can't be hollering at him. That's no way to get things done."

Jackass bent down and whispered into the opening of Tongue's window. I couldn't hear what he was saying, but his hushed tones sounded pleasant, which pissed me off even more. Then he put an ear to the crack and closed his eyes, as if listening to sea sounds in a cracked shell. I was getting more and more antsy.

"So?" I called out.

"Hush up," Jack shushed me. Then, talking to Tongue, he said, "Well, I understand that, but she's upset. And she's your friend. So why don't you just listen to what she has to say?"

Jackass put his ear to the crack again. I couldn't imagine how he was so well-versed in jumbled slobber. "Okay, okay, I'll tell her." Then to me he said, "He wants you to drop that tire iron. Thinks you're gonna clock him with it. You wouldn't do that, would you, Winnie?"

I stared at Jackass, then pitched the tire iron. I was getting tired of it. Where did this hippie get off coming between me and Tongue? I didn't like it. "Just get him out here."

"I'm doing my best," Jackass said, and he tried a new approach with Tongue.

As the horse whisperer continued to coax Tongue out of the car, I took notice of the children in the field again. They were making a real fuss trying to launch a kite into the air. They were running in a pack with a huge diamond-shaped contraption in blue, red, and yellow. There wasn't any wind, but their frustration roared out in cheers of encouragement and carefree abandonment, unlike my own, which I could hear like the hum of a choked motor inside my sternum. The irk rose inside me, and I spit out my displeasure as if coughing up a lodged hairball.

"Where's the box, Tongue? Where the fuck is it?" I threw my coiled-up body on top of the hood of Henrietta and started pounding on the windshield.

Jackass bounded back, his long hair flowing in the breeze. He wasn't prepared to cope with my kind of frantic. "Okay, okay, darlin'." He came at me with stealthy calm and tried to pull me down. I kicked out at his handsome face.

"Don't touch me." I was electric. "Back off." I was wriggling and writhing now. The pack in back stumbled out and joined Jack. They were descending upon me. They were benign, seemingly friendly, but if one of them had taken my money, I was ready to gut them all.

"Which one of you took it?" I screamed my accusation out, standing on top of the hood.

"We don't know what the hell you mean," Wayne Howl pleaded with me.

"Christ, dear, were we in your seat or something?" Burt was playing dumb like the rest of them.

Bernice had pacified Gorgy with one of Wayne Howl's drumsticks. The kid was gnawing on the bone, soothing his gums.

"There's no need for all this fussin'. It's a beautiful day," said Jackass. He regarded me differently now. My outburst had shown him something his country-cool wisdom hadn't had to contend with before. "You're out of line, missy. Would you mind telling us what you're looking for?"

"Don't play dumb," I said. "Why is the tire iron out?"

"We had a flat, darlin'." Jackass had his hands out as he approached the car, afraid I was going to try and kick him again. "We had to stop about two hours back and change her. We didn't bother to wake you because you were out cold. You sure do sleep sound."

"Are you mad that we didn't wake you?" Wayne Howl asked. He was straining to look up at me with the sun overhead. He too was moving in on me.

"This is all a bunch of fuss for nothing," Burt said, coming around the other side of me.

They were planning against me, like a pack of wolves taking down their prey. But I was above them and ready to swoop down if they gave me reason to.

"Now, come on down here, darlin'. We're all friends," said Jack.

The men were signalling to one another. I knew Wayne Howl and Burt didn't have the balls to come for me, but Jackass was working up the nerve, running his fingers through his golden locks. I saw something new in his blue eyes. They were turning beady and black.

"Stay back," I warned them. "This is my ride, and you all need to fuck off."

"Well, that's not very nice," Jackass said. "This is a big mother, and there's room for all of us."

I looked across the fields. The children had managed to launch their diamond kite. It rose into the air with a sudden burst of fury and soared above us. The string it was attached to wasn't visible from my vantage point, but I could see that it was at the mercy of the delighted children, who were making it dance. It was dancing and dancing, higher and higher. It sounds corny as hell, and it is, but I swear to Christ that I just wanted to grab hold of that diamond and have it take me away. But first, I wanted my thousands.

I tapped on the windshield with my boot. Tongue was glued to the window, tracing the movements of the kite with his huge, glowing eyes.

"Look at it," I yelled to Tongue. I knew he was loving it.

Tongue lost sight of it as it soared above us on the side of the road. The whole group looked up then at the thing above us. It was so solid in the air yet weightless. Tongue couldn't bear not seeing the flight in full, so he burst out of the car at long last.

Bernice carried her Gorgy around to the other side to get a better look. His big, puffy cheeks glistened while he sucked on the bone. Even the pack of bearded dogs around me backed off, as they too watched the solo fight of that diamond kite in the sky.

But then, in the midst of that blink of wonder, Adam's Apple, who had been hanging far away from the group, afraid that I would kick the bastard in the throat, finally spoke. He issued a bloodcurdling screech as if the apple inside him was an atom bomb going off: "Look out!"

And we saw that diamond above us evaporate in a horrific flash as it crashed into one of the monstrous electrical towers. The tower sent a line of fire across the sky, down to the fields along the length of the string that was attached to the kite. The children at the helm went silent as if the entire scene had been electrocuted. Adam's Apple instantly pissed himself and started galloping on the spot, holding onto his pecker. Bernice covered Gorgy's eyes and bolted back inside the limo. My attackers turned off me and went running to the children. Tongue was in a daze, still searching the sky for the burning diamond.

"Hey." I poked my finger into Tongue's back, and he turned around. He was wearing the saddest face in the world. His tongue hung out of his downturned mouth. "Where's the cigar box, man? Where's the money?" Tongue just looked at me, stunned. I slapped him across his face. "Snap out of it. Where's the money, Billy? Where is it?"

He looked at me and cocked his head like a retarded dog. Then he lifted up his shirt, and I saw sticking down the front of his barrel waist all the beautiful stacks of our dough tucked safely inside his big brown belt. I was so relieved that I wrapped my arms around him and kissed his hollow belly button.

"Why didn't you just say so?"

I had no intention of driving another minute with those Maritime fools. Tongue and I settled back into our rightful roles inside the limo, and I politely asked

Bernice to take her fat ass and her screaming brat out of my car. We were about to take off when Jackass came bounding back towards us, holding a screaming boy in his arms. The child's hands were blackened, and his face was wet and red from crying. Pulling up the rear were Wayne Howl and Burt, out of breath.

"Gotta get this one to the hospital." Jack too was out of breath. His chiselled face had gone white, and his long hair was messy.

The other two idiots nodded in agreement. Gorgy started up again. It wasn't my mess. I hadn't sought it out or caused it, but it had found me as it always does. Then Adam's Apple appeared. He was in the worst shape of all. He stood at the top of the hill, panting, looking as if he had something he wanted to say. He stayed that way for a few moments and then went running towards the factory. The entire time, Tongue had been searching the sky, lost. I wondered if he'd cracked up. If some of the electrical charge from the kite had shorted a circuit inside him too. Nobody seemed to know what to do. I hadn't the faintest idea where we were.

"Where the hell are we, anyway?" I asked. I wasn't about to let any of them back in the car. The kid, although terrified, looked fine. I wasn't so much against taking him somewhere, but I was still weary of the others despite having my loot secured.

"Edmundston, New Brunswick." This came from a young girl a few years older than the boy who'd been hurt. She came on the scene, strolling up the hill behind the rest of them, calmly, seemingly without care. Almost bored.

"Maybe you could just drive us home," she said. Then she went over to the boy in Jack's arms and started to look him over. "I'm sure he's fine. He's my kid brother. He's always doing stupid stuff like this. You can put him down."

Jack did, and the boy ran and hid behind his big sister. I saw an affection between the two of them that must have done some kind of number on me, as the next thing I knew, I had the whole gang (minus Adam's Apple, wherever he might have been) packed inside the back of old Henrietta, and we were taking directions on how to get to the kid's house. I didn't appreciate getting off course. I was, however, happy to learn that we'd made it to the taint of the east coast of Canada.

15

As it turned out, the fiasco in the fields initially worked out for the best. It was a bit of a lucky break depending on how you want to interpret the events that followed, but considering that I haven't laid the events out yet, and it would be a while before I could even clearly register them, I will just say that we ended up staying in Edmundston longer than planned.

We had to take the kid and his sister home. I had reclaimed my rightful place in the driver's seat with Jackass riding shotgun. Tongue kept watch on the boy in back with the others. Something was lost in the translation from the kids to Tongue to Wayne Howl to Bert and Bernice to Jack to me, and we ended up turning around about half a dozen times before finding the place. Everything was mountain range and roller coaster two-lane roads. Jack sat uneasily in his seat, keeping an eye on me to see if I'd snap again. I liked having this kind of fear in his heart.

We eventually pulled up a long driveway with a perfectly manicured front lawn containing tall looming trees and a garden with kitschy statues. The brother and sister were loaded. I stayed back in Henrietta as the kids ran to the front door of the towering brick mansion in the woods with a succession of arching bay windows and an endless white veranda. The pack of wanderers followed. Tongue was more interested in the fountain of two nymphs shooting water out of holes by the entranceway.

I lit a cigarette and watched the scene play out in front of me. The entire time, the pull for me to just drive away was strong. I'd already reclaimed my money and knew that Saint John, the city where we'd deserted Mom all those years ago, was only about four hours away.

A short, bald, stocky man wearing a bathing suit came running outside, followed by a short, stocky woman wearing a one-piece swimsuit and a bathing cap. They embraced the kids, and I was seeing double. The parents looked identical. I could see Jack spewing his charm on them, pointing to the sky, mimicking the movements of the kite before it caught fire. Then the rescue and his embellished act of heroism. His greasy hair was pulled back into a ponytail resembling a snake. The couple shook hands with the group and began to usher them all inside.

At that point, a long white limousine pulled up beside me and my long white limousine. The other car was new and sparkling, whereas mine was well past her glory days—a veritable shit box, dented and rusted and from the eighties.

The driver of the shiny one opened a window that slid down effortlessly, probably with the flick of a switch. He signalled to me. The red-faced flunky called out in a nasally voice, "What's up?"

I rolled down my window by cranking its sticky handle. A cloud of smoke plumed out. "Eh?"

"Why are you here? And who are you?" Indignant.

I got a kick out of his grimace. "Why are you here, bud?"

"Um, 'cause I'm the driver."

"No, no. I'm the driver."

The peevish prick turned beet red and pursed his lips.

"I'm your replacement," I continued. "Word is you're doing a shit job."

"Excuse me?"

"It's not okay to give hand jobs and free rides to your friends when you're off duty, pal."

"Whatever...." The prissy driver pulled away towards an enormous six-car garage.

I stepped out of Henrietta and stretched my legs. Jack motioned for me to join them in the house. I flicked my half-finished smoke into the nymph fountain before meeting Mr. and Mrs. Tweedledumdee Moneybags.

"Thank you so much for helping them get home safe," the fat woman said. "I'm Faye Stocks, and this is my husband, Reggie."

"We owe you folks," said Fat Papa. "Chet and Lola know they shouldn't be playing behind the factory. My brother runs the place for us, and he was supposed to be keeping an eye on them. But kids will be kids, I guess. You must let us thank you."

"We were just sitting down to some barbeque. Julio, our chef, grills a mean T-bone. Won't you join us?"

Tongue was licking his lips. Wayne Howl popped a boner.

"No thanks," I said.

"Please," Mama Meat persisted, "we really want to set things right."

"I'm gonna do you one better, Ma," her husband said. "Tomorrow's the day of my company's picnic and jamboree. I'd love it if you'd all be our guests." I saw their nipples hardening through their bathing suits. "Gonna be lots of fun. All kinds of rides and entertainment. Ever hear of Freewheeling Arnie and His Boom Boom Band? We booked 'em! It's gonna be a real jamboree. I close the factory once every year at the end of the summer and all the workers and all the workers' families come. And seeing as how nearly every household in these parts has somebody working for me, everyone will be there."

Fat Mama nodded enthusiastically. "A real jamboree!"

The look on Tongue's face meant that I was trapped. He would have been happy with Julio's meat, but these factory owners were promising the world, and I knew I couldn't say no. In a way, I was happy to appease

Tongue. Things hadn't been quite right between us since my last outburst. He refused to look at me since we left the field, but as he peeked over to me now, biting his bottom lip, hoping I'd say yes, as if I were in control of his movements, I knew I'd have to set up camp for the night in that mansion in the woods.

They rushed us around to the backyard and sat us down to plates of charred cow, the likes of which I'd never seen before. Big beautiful portions. Tongue ate five steaks. Wayne Howl ate three. Burt and Bernice were vegetarians, so Julio had to go in and prepare some soy burgers from scratch. After they'd filled their gullets, they stripped down and jumped into a giant kidney-shaped pool. The kids and the factory owners joined them. Tongue swam like a fish.

Jack and I had stayed behind on the deck. "So, what's your deal?" I asked him.

"My deal? The eternal question."

"Cut the shit. What are you up to?"

Jackass stared at me and then started to suck at a piece of steak caught in his teeth. "Just going with the flow. Wherever the wind takes me. Like you, I imagine."

"What do you know about me?"

"I know you kick like a mule and are just as stubborn. I know you're running from something. I know you got a box full of money and an old fancy car that's not registered. I know that you're coming off of something. Dark circles under your eyes. Mood swings. Jumpy legs. Signs are pretty clear."

"Are they?"

"I also know that you're dragging that big fella into something he shouldn't be getting into. He's like a big dumb child." Jack undid his ponytail so that his long flowing hair was free to blow in the late summer breeze. "But I can help you out, if you want me to." He reached down and pulled a small jewel-studded box from his left cowboy boot. When he clicked it open, I regarded the contents with hunger. "I think I know you better than you think."

"Yes," I said, suddenly taken by his con-man arguments, "I think we may have an understanding after all."

Jackass and I snuck away from the pool party into an upstairs bathroom and shared a few lines of some hillbilly heroin.

The stuff hit me hard.

I bounded up from the floor and opened the top-floor window to grab some air. It looked out onto the backyard playground. Tongue was standing on the diving board. He braced himself, ran forward in two lumbering strides, and vaulted. He seemed to linger endlessly, weightlessly in space before crashing down into that kidney-shaped pool, sending waves and cries of excitement into the air. The scene was streaked in brilliant rays of blue light.

16

The seven of us stayed in the factory owners' guesthouse that night. The place was larger and cleaner than any house I'd ever lived in. Burt, Bernice, and Gorgy stayed in the master bedroom, singing folk lullabies. Tongue and Jack set up camp in the room with bunk beds. The leviathan on top, and Jack on the bottom. I distinctly saw fear in Jack's wide eyes as he watched Tongue's joyous leap into the higher bed, which shook the floor. There was no way around it: The big man knew what he wanted, and he wanted to sleep closer to the heavens despite the creaking springs beneath. Even if the bunk held, Jack would have to contend with Tongue's night roars and mumbles, his snores and night songs, and the sounds that only his body could make. I hoped it would inject the beatnik with a touch of trepidation. I didn't like his swagger or how he knew about my secret stash of cash. I hated that I was now beholden to him, for he was dealing my cure, which he kept in his little jewelled box inside his boot. I think Wayne Howl was gonna sleep on the couch or the floor.

I showered for the first time in weeks inside a luxurious guest bathroom that was completely tiled in various blues. The mirror faced the clear glass-enclosed shower, and I felt uneasy looking at my naked body through the steam. I looked sickly, made all the more strange by my rich surroundings, as if I'd been brought into civilization from the wild, a newly discovered species to be experimented on. How many teeth did I have in my head? What colour was my blood? What was my core body temperature? I was a specimen in that mirror. I looked away to avoid my reflection, towelling off.

I was used to more ravaged surroundings, and although I was glad to be feeling clean for the first time in weeks, the brightness and newness of the place made me stick out—sore—even to myself. The only time I'd ever really felt like I belonged somewhere was when I spent a few months at my grandmother's house in the woods of Eastern Ontario when I was thirteen years old. She lived alone in a miraculous old shack made of mud and tires. The house was a kind of marvel in backwoods engineering.

My grandmother's name was Lois, but we all called her Ma Edna for some reason. Her first house, the one my mother grew up in, had burned to the ground. My grandfather had apparently started the fire as an insurance fraud scheme, but the idiot had neglected to keep current with his insurance payments. He was so far in arrears that his insurance claim had been cancelled unbeknownst to him. He'd slaved away his entire life in a bumper factory for thirty-five years to pay for a modest bungalow. Retirement allowed him to drink full-time, buy scratch lottery tickets, rot, and be even crueller to his family and to the squirrels that ate from his pear tree in the backyard.

As the debts mounted, he decided to torch his home. He got the idea from a newspaper cartoon featuring a family of pigs. Gumpy set the place ablaze with a book of matches and a lemonade jug filled with kerosene. The story goes from Ma Edna that he realized that his insurance claim was null and void while he stood in his pyjamas at 4 a.m. watching what he'd spent his life to build go up in flames. Naturally, he did the only logical thing: go inside his man-made inferno and try to put out the fire with a keg of Labatt Blue. It didn't work, and Gumpy melted. That's how Ma Edna ended up alone in the forest in that enchanted shack.

That was all when my parents were first married. My father and Uncle Dirk promised my mother that they would build Edna a house at a cut rate. They took her survivor money from the bumper factory and claimed that they used it to buy the railway ties and truck tires they acquired for constructing the most fucked-up abode you can imagine. It always smelled of rancid feet and wet earth. The place froze in winter, leaked in spring, and sweat in summer. But that fall, when I ran away and got to stay with Ma Edna for eight weeks, the place was just perfect. A disaster, yes, but I felt free inside its rubber rubble rooms.

Not that you could move in there. Ma Edna was the most successful hoarder in all of the Kawarthas. After the fire, she spent every waking moment filling her life with as much ruin as she could get her gnarled hands on. I suppose she was replacing the life that'd been reduced to ashes. She called all of her shit "antiques," and she fancied herself an expert collector. She didn't discriminate. She categorized her garbage not by function or date or design but by material. So glass—jars, windows, marbles, bowls, dishes, vases, pop bottles, beer bottles, wine bottles (always with the bottles)—was all kept in one pile, while metal—bicycle parts, car parts, utensils, tools, doorknobs, locks, keys, pipes, tins, pots, aluminum siding, bumpers—was all kept in another pile. I swear to God she had one of everything ever made. Paper, wood, and fabrics had all been placed together. She had a reason for this, something to do with how the stuff decayed, but I can't recall. Really, it was all just refuse she found in a nearby dump.

Every morning that I stayed with her that fall, we'd get up before dawn and put on big rubber boots and drag a grocery cart with screeching wheels about two kilometres through a path in the forest that she'd blazed herself over the years to sort through a landfill crawling with rats and a few other backwoods collectors. I never asked her, but I'm pretty sure that Ma Edna had planned on taking every last bit of trash in the junkyard and cramming it all inside her rubber hovel. And, of course, every morning brought more garbage, more waste to sort through—more remnants of people's handling, wearing, feasting, breaking, smashing, forgetting, discarding. Man, that dump was a miserable sight, but whatever we brought back to Ma Edna's, however useless or broken, had a home inside her determined heart and inside that cluttered bunker—that vermin-infested house made of rubber and dirt.

I was thinking about old Ma Edna and her antiques as I stood naked inside that pretentious bathroom inside that shiny guesthouse. Surely the rich bastards had a hefty house insurance plan. As often happens, I felt a sudden pull towards destruction. I grabbed a face cloth from a golden towel rack and flushed it down the toilet. The water backed up almost to the rim of that porcelain throne before slowly receding. I suppose I was aiming at backing up their whole drainage system and sending sewage streaming into their kidney-shaped pool. I looked around to see if there were any other traces of myself that I could leave, and I was fixing to pour the hydrogen peroxide into the bottle of shampoo when Wayne Howl opened the door, disrupting my wrecking party. His eyes bugged out of his hedgehog head, and he started licking his lips. He'd evidently never seen a naked woman before.

"I ain't seen nothing!" He had a rolled-up newspaper under his arm.

I was happy to be leaving him to contend with the clogged pipe. I gathered my pathetic pile of decaying clothes and ran past him, leaving him to his evening purge.

In the hallway, I came face to face with a kind of gallery of kitschy Canadian art. Pathetic landscape paintings in glistening oils adorned the walls. Images of Canada as seen through the fantasy lens of the rich. A kind of paint-by-numbers approach to the power of the Canuck wilderness. I scanned the ready-made pictures for any trace of Ma Edna's hut, or for the hidden factories in behind the trees of the unreal boreal forests, puffing smoke into an overbearing sky. But there was nothing but a happy family of busy beavers or a smattering of leaves colouring the forest floor. And all those goddamn loons! Some kind of an attempt at a symbol. The cry of those beasts could not be heard in the staleness of those images.

Riding high for the past few weeks, I knew that the land through Henrietta's windows held more than what this gallery was showing to me. I took out my black eyeliner from the pocket of my cut-off jeans. The paintings, I decided, needed to be fixed. The one I chose to edit was at the end of the hall: a small lakefront surrounded by mighty oak trees and a sky that opened up beyond a rock clearing. I scratched in Ma Edna's mud hut right at the centre of the lush green forest. She, alone in her cocoon with her rotting antiques hidden inside, might redeem the piece. Or so I thought as I stood there, dripping in the hallway and marking up that scene on the wall with my makeup.

The door to Jack and Tongue's room opened a crack. I let him watch me standing there, naked, defacing the forest.

17

The twenty-second annual Marrow and Tuft Mannequin Factory Employee Picnic and Jamboree took place the next day in a park by a lake. The park was the size of nine football fields. Everyone in that lumberjack town descended upon the scene, looking for a good time. Families drove up and parked on the grass, carrying blankets and lawn chairs and coolers filled with beer and potato salad. There were various tents pitched across the land, and a large bandstand was set up at the centre of the spectacle.

Also, as promised, a country carnival had been erected, which seemed to be rousing the most excitement, especially from Tongue, who was fighting the sun as he gazed up at the rickety Ferris wheel spinning. There were other rides there too: a merry-go-round, bumper cars, a Tilt-A-Whirl, and something called the Spider. The midway games were pathetic: a few pop-bottle shooting galleries, some box display called Buddy Bear, where you had to throw plastic balls into a big stuffed bear's mouth for a chance to win mood rings and bouncy balls. The usual schlock you find at any travelling amusement park that roams across the country, looking for small towns so bored and desperate for entertainment that no matter how old the rides, or how rusted, people are only too happy to give away their hard-earned money in return for tinny circus music, burned cotton candy, greasy doughnuts, and popcorn that tastes like it's been popped in motor oil.

The whole thing was something like the General Motors picnics of my childhood. My father had never worked for GM, but all his gambling buddies did. Hell, everybody in Oshawa did. So when the company picnic came up, my family would crash it, knowing that nobody would know any different. Of course, we never had any rides, just tons of chicken wings and gallons of beer. It was always so disturbing to see all those families coming out of their holes. Families who looked like my own: snot-nosed kids, overworked fathers, and hungover mothers chain-smoking and wearing tight faded blue jeans and fried hairdos. I was seeing them again from a new angle. This wasn't my town, and I wasn't related to any of them, and even though I was two provinces away, I recognized these people as phantoms from my past.

I decided that Tongue had had to put up with enough of my shit over the past few weeks and that I owed him a good time. That's why I'd stayed. I promised myself that I wouldn't ruin it for him. Besides, I bought $500 worth of first-class shit from Jack that morning, so I knew I'd be just fine.

Summer was coming to an end, so there was an extra charge surging through those fields. It was the last few days of freedom for the children before going back to school. It must have been tough for all those families at the jamboree to survive the summer because this pack was looking rather wretched as they swarmed the fair grounds. It was exhausting just looking at them breathe. I could see the toll of getting up every day and carving out a measly speck of life. They all seemed so caustic, fighting a burning August sky and an impatient autumn wind. Desperate too, for fun, for food, for beer, for rides to go faster. Everyone was clamouring to get their turn on those stupid rides, which were all just variations on a jagged circle. I was getting a headache watching them go round and round, wearing sad smiles on their faces. No one was having a good time. No one could convince me otherwise.

Even Tongue seemed a bit bewildered by it all. Too many choices for him, I suppose. At least he was tall enough to go on any ride he wanted. I loaded him up with one of every rancid treat they were hawking. Bought him a handful of balloons too because he couldn't decide on his favourite colour.

Most kids were bitching to their parents for more of everything. You had to buy tokens to take part in any of the attractions, a way for the factory owners to turn a little profit on company fun day. Most moms weren't able to or didn't want to dish out enough coin to appease all their frantic, freckled, freak kids'

appetites. But I was. I gave Tongue a hundred bucks. He found a discarded bucket that some family had kept their bean salad in, and we filled the thin
g with tons of shiny copper tokens. As we were doing so, an overprotective mother, clearly uneasy about being there, walked by us with her child, who was strapped in a harness at the end of a leash. I wondered what kind of saddle I'd need to rein in my boy, Tongue.

The only ride I agreed to go on was the bumper cars. I always loved the bumper cars. My family went up to Toronto one summer to squeeze ourselves into the Canadian National Exhibition, the infamous CNE. My dad was desperate for work that year, and one of his bowling teammates got him a gig as a part-time carnie. I'd wished he'd run away and join the circus permanently. The job meant that my brothers and I could go to the fair every day for free, or so we thought.

My old man was manning the bumper cars, which was a kind of miracle for me. Instead of getting us a babysitter, he took us with him to work and let us ride those cars all day long, smashing into one another at what felt like breakneck speeds. Ramming one another. It was when the boys and I would turn our attacks on other kids that I really got off on the derby. Because we had so much practice, it wasn't long before we were experts. Whenever Dad let on the next batch of riders, my brothers and I would work together, corner some little brat and have at him.

It was the only time I can remember really getting

along with the boys. I suppose I was just happy that for once I wasn't at the short end of their bullying. Our greatest victory that day was when Pop had to tend to a broken-down car. The idiot kept the ride going as he jumped into the arena to dislodge some prissy kid who had managed to get himself stuck. When my brothers and I saw our father in the ring, we all set our sights on his poorly fitting uniform—those baggy navy-blue coveralls and muddy Kodiak work boots with the laces untied.

We smashed the hell out of Dad that day, sent him bouncing in all directions. Onlookers were horrified and started calling out for us to stop, but that wasn't an option. Really, the old fool was getting off on it. He was fair game as far as we all were concerned—no mercy, just like the old bastard taught us. Take the chance, whatever chance presents itself, and don't back down. One of the other carnival attendants eventually saw what was going on and shut down the ride. I didn't see how it was any different from the kind of freak shows that regularly played out at our house. Dad got his hand crushed. It swelled up to the size of a catcher's mitt. It meant that it'd hurt every time he'd swat at us. He was fired when they found out he'd been letting his kids onto rides for free. I hadn't been in a bumper car since.

I still wasn't able to shake the hitchhikers. We walked together through the picnic grounds in a group. Burt and Bernice were wearing matching khaki shorts and safari hats with strings that tied under their chins. Wayne Howl had stayed up late making peanut butter and maple syrup sandwiches, and he'd already managed to completely smear himself in glop by the time we made it to the bumper cars. I was looking forward to smashing them all. Especially Jackass, who had somehow become the leader of our pack.

Everyone liked him, and he knew how to control you in a way that was non-threatening. It was his big phony smile and smarmy laugh, the way his luscious hair bounced, and the way he could stare you down that made it hard to resist what he was saying. Pure puke positivism. I'd fallen for similar tyrants before—those who never wore their manipulations on the surface. It was hard to detect Jack's stronghold, but I had. I'd catch him looking at me from time to time, and whenever our eyes met, he'd wrinkle his forehead and flash some toothy knowing grin as a reminder that he knew the high that I was riding was one that he'd provided. Goddamn the pusher man. I looked forward to ramming him the most. But when our turn finally came, after waiting in an obnoxious line for twenty minutes, I lost my chance.

This carnival was so chintzy that they made you ride two people per car. Unless you were Tongue, who could barely squeeze himself inside alone, you had to pick a partner. Burt and Bernice were attached at the hip, and I wasn't gonna get anywhere near Jack or get myself glued to Wayne Howl's sticky thighs, so I had to back out. Bernice handed Gorgy over to me like she was tossing over a sack of rotten potatoes. I was pretty sure he'd filled his diaper.

Tongue was so excited about showing off his new driving skills that it wasn't until they were all strapped in and the tyrannical music started playing that he saw that I'd been left behind, made to stand on the sidelines, holding onto a squirmy Gorgy. Tongue's knees were forced up to his chin because he was so large, and he looked over to me, excited at first, just before getting rear-ended by a hooting Jackass. Tongue must have known how I felt at that moment because his eyes slitted with rage. He stuck his tongue out and set off in a jerk, looking for revenge.

I'd never actually held a baby before. Wrestling with my kid brother didn't count, and, besides, whenever Pete and I would grapple, I'd usually end up just holding him upside down by his ankles. Little Gorgy was a pudge. His soft body felt awkward in my grip. I didn't know how to hold on without feeling that I'd leave bruises. His baby fat seemed far too mushy for my boney hands and arms, which were all the more mechanical because of how he was crawling all over me and breathing. I could feel his little heart beating away like a bird's flutter or the whirl of a tiny perfect propeller. I had to admit that the little shit was cute. He started pulling on my ears, and our faces met. I had one arm under his soggy butt and my other arm supporting his wayward head. It seemed so damn precarious bobbing around. He was making grimaces. As if he were trying to get a reaction out of me. Then he stuck a few fingers inside his wet mouth and started slobbering, drooling like a baby bulldog. He didn't have any teeth and so gummed on his tiny tongue, spitting and babbling away, all the while arching his back and dancing in my arms.

I was paralyzed by that child. I felt useless. As useless as I'd ever felt. Diminished. Gorgy's little body held complete command over me. It was all that I could do not to drop him. The buzzing in my head and the whirling of the rides around us was anchoring me to the ground. I felt like a sharp spike hammered down into supple earth. The kid hiccupped and spit up his mother's breast milk onto my shoulder. Was I supposed to burp him? Pat him? Rock him? Kiss him? He started crying. I felt his diaphragm rise and quiver as he let out piercing notes. I had no way of knowing what he wanted. He was a bouncing ball of need—a breathing, puking lump of want. Change him? Sing to him? He wanted his mother, that's what he wanted. I wanted to run away.

It occurred to me then, as it had periodically since I was a teenager, that some stranger in this big blue world had cared for my own child, had given my baby comfort and milk and watched him grow. And if I found him now, or if I ever found him, I knew he would no longer be a baby, and I knew that his needs would have grown and that he had never needed me and would never need me. Gorgy was a ghostly reminder of the son they ripped out of me decades ago.

Whom I'd always wanted, always needed. As the perfect mess of a child cried in my arms, my whole body ached. Tears started gushing from my eyes. Snot ran from my nose. I wanted to puke too. Gorgy and I were a puddle standing on the sidelines. We were drenching one another in fluids, and neither of us cared.

Tongue's rampage in the ring was getting a lot of attention. I had taught him well. I'd never seen him so aggressive. I was proud to see him smash his competition. He slunk his car marvellously around the makeshift battleground and had at them all. The hitchhikers' initial excitement had been traded in for frustration and fear as the giant relentlessly stalked and attacked. His brilliance jolted me out of my momentary descent into despair, and I began to shout words of real encouragement to my big strong boy. I felt like a crazed soccer mom screaming on the pitch. Tongue could send them all over the moon. Unstoppable. He was an unleashed bull bucking all and anyone who stood in his way. The rodeo continued to play out that way for me, only for me, and I was glad for it.

18

Evening brought a different kind of fun as the sun descended and turned into a huge red candy apple crawling with worms. Tongue and I were alone, at last, though surrounded by a village of tuckered-out workers and their families. I wanted to hit the road and get the hell out of there and told Tongue so. But he was insatiable. He wanted to stay, even though all the rides had wound down and he'd eaten all there was to swallow. The place was all in a tizzy because Freewheeling Arnie and His Boom Boom Band were about to take the stage. We were making our way toward a field in the far west end of the park. I was happy to be moving away from the children and the midway.

There was a string of tents surrounding the bandstand, where a crack team of sound technicians were checking levels and adjusting lights. A crowd began to form and spread out on blankets and lawn chairs. Someone had been drilling a hole in my head all day, and I longed for it to be filled in with cement. It was so depressing to see all those middle-aged rockers squeezed into tight-fitting leather pants and faded tee shirts, all hoping to relieve their glory days—pockmarked and high in the seventies.

Plumes of pot smoke wafted above the heads of the concertgoers. I wondered if Jackass was selling loose joints. We'd parted ways a few hours earlier. I sincerely hoped to never see him or his long, greasy hair again. All of the hitchhikers were sore at Tongue for turning them into mice at the mercy of his great catlike pounces. Good riddance. The incident with Gorgy had confirmed it: I needed to find my son. My father had placed his baby picture in the cigar box, knowing that it would shake and rattle me, and it had. I thought that the pain of those days had been sufficiently buried and that I'd built a life out of the charred remains, but judging by the way the images of it all were flashing acid in my brain, I hadn't buried it deep enough. (Could I really still smell the scent of his tiny precious head?) It was all coming up now. I was spitting it up like Gorgy's sour milk.

Thunderous hoots and hollers ushered Arnie on stage. They freaking loved him. The Boom Boom Band kicked in. Arnie was at least sixty, although it was hard to tell from my vantage point. He was squat, hairy, puffy, and manic. He started shaking his head back and forth in time with the thumping bass drum. As he did, his long brown hair sprayed the audience with sweat. He was a crazed briar patch, complete with thistles and brambles. Then he started a fierce yodel. The crowd responded with matched ferocity. Old Brambles began to perform somersaults and one-handed cartwheels. This even impressed me.

Tongue was out of control. He held his powerful arms in the air, pumping his fists. "Boom boom boom boom boom boom!"

Some emaciated fiddler burst out of nowhere and started to saw himself a screeching path through the air, his arm on fire. Arnie settled himself, still stomping his foot, at the centre of the stage. He made to talk into the microphone and was met with a blast of deafening feedback. He scowled, stuck his tongue out, and gave the microphone the middle finger. When the hack sound techs finally fixed it, all our ears were bleeding, and still they chanted: "Boom boom boom boom boom!"

The band launched into a bluegrass version of "Born to Be Wild," which began with a harmonica solo from the wild man himself.

Tongue was over the moon, and I was glad to see him having such fun, but I couldn't stand it much longer.

"Gonna go get something to drink..." I told him. But he couldn't hear me over the ruckus; he was somewhere else. Saliva ran down his chin. He'd been transported by Arnie's irrepressible showmanship and the frenzy of the crowd. I didn't want to spoil this party, so I escaped into one of the massive tents nearby. Because of the headache, I felt justified in popping nine Percs, which seemed to take the edge off a little.

The tent was a catch-all for various activities, which I observed through my sudden sympathetic haze. There was a swap meet of sorts at the far end. A bunch of bored blue-hairs sat hunched over their wares, selling moldy-looking antiques: costume jewelry, furniture, books, old cigarette cases, lace tablecloths, candle holders, china, gas station signs, broken toys, old magazines—a whole whack of crap.

I wandered past a lady with whiskers who tried to sell me a bronze medallion in the shape of a frog. She held the thing up in the air, wheezing and screaming, "Make me an offer!"

Next, I made my way over to the hot dog eating contest set up by the baked goods. Three serious-faced fatties were doing mouth exercises in preparation for the games to begin, opening their traps as wide as they could and breathing deeply. I knew Tongue could beat them all without trying, but he'd never leave the concert now. Arnie and the Boom Boom boys were playing a country version of "A Wonderful World."

A man made out of melted butter and wearing a cat sweater blew a whistle, and the contestants started to hoover down dog, gorging themselves on wiener. They each had their own techniques. The one on the left with a chinstrap beard and high hair dunked his hotdogs, bun and all, into a cup of orange juice before cramming it inside his hole. The guy beside him just crammed them in dry as bits of bun flew everywhere. He kept trying desperately to breathe though his piggy nose. The third contestant was taking great care to dress each hotdog with relish and mayonnaise before putting it back, humming as he did so. Still, he was able to pack one in every thirty seconds or so. It took me a few minutes to realize that it was none other than Wayne Howl. All 210 pounds of the silly slop man. I was glad that I hadn't recognized him at first. It meant that his ugly mug had not yet permeated my brain.

As I passed by that hogfest, I took heart in knowing two things: one, I'm pretty sure Howl was choking to death; and two, I'd already erased him from my mind even before I'd ever met him. Most people were like that for me—apparitions. Perhaps this vacuum effect was some form of survival I'd picked up along the way, the ability to turn people into handfuls of ash. Or else it was because my mind was already stuffed with haunted faces and there was no more room for ghouls inside me.

I wanted to be alone, but going around behind the tents, I found a mud-wrestling tournament. Drunk men stood around a pit, watching brutish women grunt and snort and pull hair in slime. The ladies were wearing white tee shirts that showed hard nipples poking through. The degenerates around the ring pounded their beer bellies with fists clutching five dollar bills, making bets on who was going to come out on top. On a good day, I could have whooped both Magnificent Mavis and Freaky Franca no problem. I'd be Whipper Winnie Watson.

In eleventh grade, I beat the snot out of Mr.

Lafontaine. Like most gym teachers, he was bald, fat, dumb, and mean-spirited. His wife also taught at our shitty high school. She was my actual phys ed teacher. I'm pretty sure she was a dyke, and I'm pretty sure she thought that I was one too. Mrs. Lafontaine called in sick one day, and her dick husband came in to sub for our class. Probably not getting any action at home, the depraved prick was only too happy to look after a group of sixteen-year-old gals sweating in short shorts. We were supposed to be finishing up a unit in dodge ball, but Lafontaine started setting up the wrestling mats instead, blathering something about discipline.

It was tough for me being the kid sister of the McKeagan boys. My brothers had all been expelled for various reasons over the years. Ralph stole the school mascot and pushed him into the creek. Randy had sex with Miss Price, the secretary. Liam had sex with Ms. Glenda, the school nurse. Duncan had a thing for pissing on the blackboards. As a result, I was treated poorly by the staff. Revenge for all the years of hell my brothers had put them all through. I wasn't much better myself, I guess. Smoking in the bathroom kind of stuff. I was bored out of my mind most of the time.

That morning, I was still recovering. My stomach was killing me. It always comes back to the pain in my gut. I told this to Lafontaine, and he told me to suck it up. He didn't like slackers. I walked the track instead of running for warm-up, and this seemed to enrage him. He paired off all us girls, except for me, and told us to start grappling. My idiot, naïve classmates were loving it. They couldn't understand that the pervert just wanted to see teenage girls touching one another, grunting and rolling around.

After about ten minutes of squealing, Lafontaine had a pathetic bulge in his sweatpants, and he gathered the class in a circle for a demonstration. In an effort to teach me a lesson, I suppose, he told me to get down on all fours. I complied. But the second I felt his wet, meaty body next to me on the mat, I elbowed him hard in the teeth. He knelt holding onto his bloody mouth, and I leapt to my feet and started to kick him in the ribs, hard. The girls started to cry.

He was the first man I'd wrestled with besides my father, but it felt just as satisfying. The difference here was that whenever I'd pound on Dad, he'd be drunk. Lafontaine was sober. I knew enough not to tangle with my father without a few drinks in him first. I had the advantage over Lafontaine in this case because I'd taken him by surprise and exploded on the moron, but it wasn't long before he regained his footing and tackled me to the ground, hard. He held me down while some of the girls ran for help.

Mavis and Franca weren't really fighting up to my standards. I could see that this was more of a tit show for the men than an honest bout. It seemed rehearsed. Franca had her thighs around Mavis' head in a tight scissors lock. She let out a scream. Then Franca flipped her. The two Clydesdales landed on their backs, whacked in the mud.

"Pin her! Pin her!" The spectators were hoarse.

A gangly kid, the referee, scrambled inside the pigpen. Mavis rolled her large body on top of Franca for the three count. I got the hell out.

I stumbled back to the concert. The stage was sagging in the middle. I couldn't find Tongue at first. He wasn't where I'd left him. But looking up to the stage, I found him, all right. He'd joined Arnie front and centre, and the two were crooning a heartfelt rendition of Dylan's "Just Like a Woman." The crowd accepted the giant even though he spat at the entire first row every time he hit the words "just like." He had his arm around Brambles, and the two were swaying back and forth, conducting the nausea of the crowd, who held up their lighters. Everyone was too drunk and weepy now to care that we were being eaten alive by blackflies.

I headed back to Henrietta to sleep it off. I couldn't be sure what was real or imagined anymore. Sufficiently wrecked.

Now, I never asked for the following horror. I never sought it out, any of it. I never even asked to be born. I swear to Christ it finds me. It crawls through the overgrown grass, slithers like a snake, and wraps itself around me. For when I opened the door to my father's car, Jack was bearing fangs, banging some teenage blonde girl in the back seat. No longer his charming self. The girl, startled, starting screaming from my intrusion and covered up her bare breasts. Jack ordered me out. But I wouldn't go. He was naked except for his cowboy boots. His long hair was pulled back into a tight ponytail. I told Mitsy to beat it, and Jack breathed deeply. I suppose he thought I wanted to cut in, but I'm not that kind of dance partner. Instead, I started to slap him, hard, and Mitsy took off. Hard, like when it ricochets back up your wrist. Hard, like when you can hear the smack of a dead fish going belly up in the creek.

All revved up, Jack thought that this was some sort of twisted foreplay of mine. I slapped that dirtbag repeatedly, in the face at first, but soon all over every inch of his hard, glistening body. He started to laugh at me, when the tussling had turned him on. But it wasn't long before he felt the fire of my open palm and began to fight back. I wanted him humiliated. I wanted to slap him senseless. But really, I just wanted to slap somebody, hard.

I don't know what I expected from him. Of course he fought back. Overpowered me. His hurt pride and stinging buttocks demanded it. We didn't speak, but the struggle between us was clear, and we knew it wasn't going to end well. I wanted to overpower him, and he wanted to overpower me. It's always this way—the natural order. He ripped my shirt open. I suppose I could plead that he was trying to fondle me, but there was nothing in it for him. I was the aggressor despite being held down beneath his naked body.

I'm still not completely clear on the particulars of what happened next, or maybe I just choose not to recount them in full detail. Maybe my desire to do what I wanted to him and what I actually did to him morphed too grotesquely in my brain so that I will never be completely clear on what happened. The base facts of what I knew then will suffice here: I cut Jack's penis off with Tongue's Swiss Army knife. I don't remember doing it. I don't remember the mess or how loud the man howled, although there would have been plenty of both. And I certainly don't remember what I did with the thing afterwards either. Maybe I started to erase him and his thing from my mind the instant I flashed the blade through the air. Either way, he was as good as pulverized, and I got the hell out of Edmundston.

19

Tongue and I quit the freak show and its worshippers soon after, and we drove all night. It was endless forest and rolling roads for the most part. I had my foot pressed hard on the gas as Henrietta chugged and gurgled her way through the Appalachian ridge. It was good to be back behind the wheel again, and I was grateful for the road's sobering calm and the way the yellow centre line burned an arrow into my battered brain, pointing east with only a vague direction known. Tongue was stretched out in the back. He'd grown hoarse from singing at the concert. I didn't tell him about my wrestling match with Jack. The adventure had left him with a pretty bad sunburn. I spent the trip listening to him whimper as he tossed and turned against the sticky leather seats.

He awoke with the morning light as we rolled into Saint John. The entire place had been painted up in pastels. I imagined that that's what it would look like under the ocean. Tongue was intrigued by the soft colours too. By the mist. It was all fog and drizzle, and we enjoyed the feel of it on our faces with the windows down. I slowed to a crawl through the empty 5 a.m. streets. We were moving in a kind of dream state, so very quiet and hard to see. I'm sure it was exhaustion taking over or a pleasant comedown off of whatever I'd last ingested, but whatever it was, it was peace and salt water.

We pulled into a deserted waterfront overlooking a rocky cove. It felt as though it was where the earth ended and the water took over, and I wondered if we'd have to swim the rest of the way. Surrounded by rocks that had been placed randomly by the rowdy work of prehistoric gods. It was a primitive playground full of a natural violence as the water smashed against the jagged entrance to the earth. Everything was frothing as the waves overlapped and competed with each other to strip down the fishermen's caves into sand. Some kind of mad wharf. In that instant, I longed to live inside the rock with Tongue, who, out in the morning sun, looked like a bonafide leaping sea monster.

He stripped down naked and bounded towards the water. He made me laugh despite the fact that I didn't feel real in that moment. The contrast of his farmer's tan was alarming. He was a giant spinning barber pole. There was a stark contrast between the bright-red sun-soaked parts—his face, ears, neck, and arms—and the whiteness of the rest of him, especially his big, pale, bouncing buttocks. What was this strange and magnificent creature so full of wonder and innocence? It seemed so honest in its deformity. It was so clearly made of the earth. I watched it enter the water until it became indistinguishable from it. I watched it splashing around in the dazzling blue like an overgrown child. The ocean yielded to it. The creature cut through with massive strokes until it was so far out there that I began to worry it wouldn't be able to find its way back, but I knew better than to doubt Tongue.

When he emerged from the undercurrent to suck back the air, catch his breath, and blow it out like a sperm whale through his blowhole, he let out a call of pure joy that I couldn't translate into any language of logic other than the deep, pure voice of primitive happiness. He was so very alive. And I wondered why such a beautiful monster of life would have any time, let alone compassion, for me, for such a mechanical perversion of a woman. My hands and feet went numb. When had the blood in my veins stopped flowing?

I was well into this kind of common self-loathing, so deep and disappearing, when the man I call Tongue emerged from the ocean and began his walk towards me.

"You're covered in seaweed and sand."

And he seemed glad to be, or at least delighted, as he began to move his strong hands across his chest and legs, removing the remnants of his bath. I wondered if a fish or two had swum inside his belly button. He cocked his head to the side and started banging on it to unclog his ear.

"You want to go looking for buried treasure?"

He did.

Tongue put his pants back on and rolled the cuffs up to his knees. He tied his shirt around his head like a big bandana, to look more like a pirate, I presumed. He tied the laces of his boots together and hung them around his neck. If nothing else, this monster was adaptable to every situation. But it was more than that: He wanted to do everything that there was to do.

We walked along the shore in silence, and Tongue filled his pockets with pebbles and shells. Then he popped a rock inside his mouth and started to suck on the stone. By the time we made it to the fishermen's caves, his cheeks were bulging as much as his pants.

"I don't know if we should go in. Looks freaky."

But Tongue ventured inside anyway, and I followed. It was cold and dark, and it hid us perfectly. I didn't see a reason why we should ever leave. We could have made a home for ourselves there inside the rock with the water trickling in at our feet and running down the uneven walls. I preferred darkness anyway. Tongue caught his voice bouncing back at him and loved the magic of the echo. He began to sing to me. Drone.

It was hard to believe I'd made it. We were close, and I could feel it. Of course, I remembered it all differently. There were no enchanted chambers by the ocean when we abandoned Mom when I was a kid. Memories usually distort the truth, expand environments, and when you return to the real structures of your past to see them in the flesh, you find them so much smaller, duller, more muted than how they've existed in your head. But being back in that place, I found the opposite. Of course, I still needed to find the hospital, but I was surrounded now by brilliance so irrepressibly large that it stunned me. The ocean was expansive and endless. There was more on the horizon than I could fit or could have ever fit inside my battered imagination.

"This is the place."

"Yeah?"

"Not this cave exactly but close to it. It's got to be."

I was suddenly charged up. Maybe it was because I felt close to some answers. Maybe it was because I'd cut a man to pieces. Maybe I wanted nothing more than just to tell Mom that Dad was dead. Whatever it was, I was all heated up, and this high was natural. I felt alive in the mouth of the earth.

"Don't you get it? We did it. We made it. She's here."

Tongue looked bewildered.

"Who?"

"My mother. Haven't you been listening?"

I could see him puzzling through all that I'd told him. Bless his big heart. He just breathed heavily and kept his eyes locked to mine. He deserved so much better than me and my madness. I was sorry for all that I'd put him through, even though he didn't seem any worse off for it. I wondered if he knew what kind of menace he'd been riding with.

I'm not sure what I expected. Just because we had reached the eastern shores didn't mean there was a road sign pointing to the loony bin. Still, I felt close to her, maybe for the first time ever—certainly closer than I'd ever been before.

20

The red rusted bathtub of a boat we boarded that morning was aptly named *The More or Less* after the ship's sea-drunk and -drenched owners, Lester and Morella McFarland. I didn't exactly know what we were getting into, although their advertisements on the dock were hard to miss.

Morella had been braying out across the wharf, trying to reel in customers as she banged two tin pots together. While Lester, her ever-diminishing husband, stood beside her, wearing a placard and feebly playing a pennywhistle. None of the other fishermen paid them any notice. The few locals on the boardwalk seemed impervious to their spectacle. But no sooner had we come close enough to read Lester's sign than Morella pounced on us, entreating us to come aboard her vessel for a day of fishing in the Bay of Fundy and a tour of the harbour.

The woman was impossible to resist. Not only did she keep you from getting a word in with her constant jovial talk and cackle; she also continuously circled us with a kind of dance step as she beckoned us. What I found the most miraculous about Morella was her size. She was so big that she even seemed to diminish Tongue. The lady stood a stout six and a half feet and must have weighed 350 pounds. More than that, for however terrifying her exuberance came across, she had the fattest, happiest, rosiest cheeks and kindest face I'd ever laid eyes on. I couldn't help following her in whatever she asked of us.

For his part, Lester must have long since been bested by his buoyant bride, as he kept a blank expression planted on his kisser and refused to look at anyone. His eyes were fixed up and to the right as he whistled out a maritime tune. He was a few inches shorter than me and so completely dwarfed by his woman. Apart from the faintest hint of a beer gut on him, this shy little man was all bone and blisters.

Tongue was wary of them at first. Torn, ultimately, because he wanted on that boat badly, but he'd surely never met anyone like Morella before. Never been face to face (and what a face) with someone as imposing. And a lass, no less.

When it was clear that there wouldn't be any more paying customers that morning, the music stopped, and our hosts ushered us inside the cabin. Morella put away her pots, broke out a bottle of Irish whiskey, and took a long hard swill before starting up the engine. I knew right away that it was going to be an eventful voyage.

Lester buzzed around the deck, fussing with ropes and preparing nets. Tongue was anxious to get going.

Let there be whales! As Morella taxied us out of the harbour past similar fishing boats (although none with so much character), Lester brought us worn-out life jackets. Mine was too big for me, and Tongue's was too small for him, and Morella laughed and smacked and loved the fact that they didn't fit. She mocked her husband for his failed attempt at keeping us safe and said, "There ain't no need for them jackets with old Mor at the wheel anyway." She ordered Les to take them away and bring us something to drink. I could see that big Mor and I were gonna get along just fine.

When Les came back with a couple of light beers, the two of them began their bickering, which wouldn't end the entire time we were at sea with them. Mor said Les was a useless bird pecker who couldn't throw a party if his arsehole was on the line. Les said Mor had more hot air in her than all the winds in heaven. Then Mor told Les to go and get the good hooch or else she'd squash him. Les did what he was told, and by the time we were far enough away from land to not see or remember land anymore, I too was a drunken sailor.

Mor turned the boat's engine off, and Les heaved an anchor out, which plunked and sank into the dark grey water. For such a scrawny guy, he was pretty strong. Mor told Tongue to go out and help him, as he was otherwise liable to fall in again. And she cackled, recounting the time when her husband had last gone overboard while trying to pull up a net. Les grumbled out on deck, not wanting to relive the episode. Mor got redder and redder in the face as she described his spindly legs in the air and how she had to fish him out. I thought that the lady was going to blow a gasket or pee her pants. She howled, proclaiming what fools men are, how simple and useless.

Tongue seemed to even things out for poor browbeaten Les. There was no way Tongue couldn't keep up with the physical demands of the sea. As he began to pull on the ropes that Les struggled with, the old man looked at him with sincere admiration, as if finally, at long last, someone had come who could give his old lady a run for her money. Finally, someone to stand up to her brute strength.

Seeing Les pout, Mor stifled herself, although I could see she was still pleased as punch at the memory. She barked out apologies to her husband and remarked how sensitive he could be. "Sorry for bringing it up, Pa." "Sorry for playing games in front of the guests, Pa." And slowly I saw the power shift as Les refused to acknowledge what Mor was now saying to him. As is usually the way, the passive aggressor won. Les maintained his cold shoulder and held his ground, refusing to look back in Mor's direction, knowing full well that his wife couldn't stand being ignored. Instead, he took his time to instruct Tongue on the finer points of fishing in the Atlantic—something, I admit, I had no interest in at all.

"Where'd you find that one, eh?" Morella asked me. "Christ, he's a specimen. Is he big all over? I can't imagine what that tongue can do. Lordy, Lordy. Old noodle neck out there ain't called Les for nothing, you know." And she gestured at the diminutive size of her husband's member. "With that hunk of man around, I could have me some real fun."

I didn't know what to say about Tongue, how to describe him. Really, I hated the idea that Mor was lusting after him, but I knew she meant no harm. I couldn't picture him as a sexual creature. He was beyond sex, or at least beyond what I knew of the act. "He's quiet...."

"Grand! I like 'em that way. Quiet and hung like a hippo!" Mor howled some more.

"A bit slow, you know?"

"Crikey! A halfwit? And you took him as a lover anyway?"

I wasn't making myself clear. It dawned on me then that I had only recently started to understand that I had a relationship with Tongue at all. That is, we'd been together nearly every minute since we met, since he just appeared out of thin air on my doorstep, and I hadn't had to question our connection as something real. But as Mor continued to grill me, I felt tremendously possessive and protective of the man.

"It's not like that," I tried to explain to the nymphomaniac. "He's special, and I don't just mean his size and that tongue. He's unlike anyone I've ever met."

But as I continued to fumble over some sappy sentiment, Mor stopped me with a slap on the shoulder and told me to stop puzzling and getting all serious, as we hadn't come out to sea to bare our souls but to fill our holes, and she raised her bottle up high.

"I can see he's a unique character." She downed some more whiskey, and we joined our men out on the deck to do some whale watching.

Tongue remained standing the entire time, clutching the railing at the bow, his eyes glued to the water. Each time he thought he spotted one, he'd push his shoulders back and arch himself forward. But after two long hours of staring, we still hadn't seen so much as a fin or blowhole. Tongue was clearly disappointed, but he perked up when Les said it was time to check on the nets.

Wide-eyed and full of wonder, Tongue began to pull. We were all filled with anticipation as he heaved the net in closer, and we let out whoops and cheers at what we saw come out of the ocean. Mor and Les were in awe. They'd been hoping for some mackerel or haddock, or at the very most a crab or two. But Tongue had somehow managed to catch lobster on his very first try, using a net no less. How was it possible? I was a bit grossed out by all of those tentacles and squirming hard-cased bodies, but I knew better than to show any squeamishness in front of Mor and Les. They were both dumbfounded by the truly biblical proportions of Tongue's haul. Tiny miracles were child's play for him. He'd sweep the ocean floor clean if they wanted him to.

"This is a full week's earnings, my boy. You done good; you done real good!" Mor shook her head in disbelief and marvelled at the virgin fisherman. His real prowess was slowly dawning on her. She jumped up and embraced him, groping him a little, and Tongue embraced her back, and they swayed back and forth like two wrestlers from the thirties. Mor planted a wet, sloppy kiss on his cheek.

"With this one pulling gold up like this, we could finally do it, Les. We could get out once and for all!"

"Couldn't agree with you more, Mor. Couldn't agree with you more."

And the two of them stared at Tongue and licked their lips. He was their meal ticket.

The proposition was simple. Mor and Les were sick to death of life on the sea. According to Mor, they were soaked through to the bone. They'd been born by the water, were married by the captain of a clipper ship, and had lived their whole lives catching fish, and they wanted to go somewhere and dry out. Literally. They dreamed of living in the desert. They'd be damned if they were gonna die on a fishing boat. They wanted to get as far away from water and Canada's harsh winters as they could. And they were tired of eating fish to boot.

As they laid out their dream vision, I started to understand the vehemence of their crackpot business and campaign. It'd been a shoddy season on the water, so they'd taken to giving boat tours as a way to bulk up business. They were only ten thousand bucks away from getting out for good and moving to Cairo. As they told us of their need for a dry climate and their collective longing to see the pyramids, I saw the real affection between this odd couple. It was in the way they looked at one another working on this dream of escape. They were very much in love, and their fantasy was very much alive. Although I couldn't picture these two riding camelback through the desert, I was glad for them that they could.

It was in this spirit of catching fish and sharing delusions that I told them about my own quest. Of how I'd come to their harbour. Hearing it out loud made it sound reasonable. I wanted to reconnect with my past. That's why I'd come to the eastern shores. Forget the mania and self-destruction, forget the binges and rehab, forget the irrepressible longing to find justice; I was just a woman who had lost touch with her family. The story suddenly seemed so dull and uneventful, so common. Of course, I didn't mention the box of cash or the limo or the butchered drug-dealing beatnik in Edmundston.

According to Mor and Les, my task was straightforward. I needed to track down that hospital, and they could help. It sounded reasonable. It also sounded reasonable to suggest that Tongue needn't hang around for that portion of my search, that he'd probably just get in the way or get bored. Besides, he was having such a grand time with Mor and Les on the water. Or maybe I had convinced myself of all of this. I was certainly intrigued by their offer to help.

"I may know the place," Les piped in. "My cousin Shep used to work as a janitor in an institution by the

Reversing Falls. He was a janitor there for years. Of course, it's no longer running. If it's the one you want, he might be able to get you in to look around."

According to Les, the Gumble Health Centre lay boarded up on Lancaster Avenue only twenty minutes from the harbour. When our tour was finished, he'd call up Shep and make the arrangements. I was equally thrilled and terrified at the prospect. What happens when you come face to face with what haunts you? I suppose I'd never quite believed my own memory. It was a story, like so many, that I'd been telling myself for years, but I'd always reserved a glimmer of doubt. Somewhere inside me, I never completely believed myself in order to protect myself. As if somewhere deep inside, I had convinced a small part of me that I'd made the whole thing up. To suddenly be so close to flesh-and-blood proof threatened to send me over the edge of my imagination. When delusion manifests in real life, and phantoms step out of the shadows, they force you to confront yourself, your true self, and I was pretty sure I'd run away screaming.

So Mor and Les were willing to help me in my struggle to be free. As a trade-off, I'd have to surrender Tongue.

"We'll keep him safe and well-fed. Give him to us for one month."

I hated the idea that he was something that I could give away or use to trade. I told them I needed to think it over. But there wasn't much to think about. I knew

Tongue couldn't go any further with me.

By the time the winds came up and night fell upon the water, I'd made up my mind: I would leave him with Mor and Les.

"How's about we spend the night on the ocean?" Mor suggested. "You two will love it. No charge."

I think she may not have trusted herself to get us back safely. She'd been pounding the liquor into herself all day. Les didn't like the idea and began to complain about his lumbago, which set Mor off on another torrent of words: "Your mama told me you were nothing but a mewling, puking baby before I married ya. Buck up and quit complaining or I'll feed you to the seagulls in the morning."

"Yeah? Well, Mama told me that one day I'd find myself in the belly of a whale, meaning you, your belly."

They resumed their vicious play for a while, but it wasn't long before they traded in their rough work for cooing and groping in one of the tiny compartments in the cabin. I wondered how Tongue would be able to get along with these two pirates for a whole month.

"You okay if I leave you with them?"

"Sure."

Tongue had been at peace since he'd pulled in his ninth catch. I knew he liked the idea of pulling up what was hidden beneath the shimmering waters. And in my mind I knew he was exactly where he ought to be. Or anyway, I hoped he was. Even still, it didn't keep the guilt from welling up inside me. I knew that if I left him, there was a good chance we'd never see each other again.

"Both have work to do."

"Yup."

I loathed myself, but I carried on while he maintained his grip on the moon. It was dancing on the tide to a hypnotic rhythm. It was hard for me to say anything else. My own tongue had stopped working as a lump of sediment formed in my throat and my chin quivered. It wasn't withdrawal or seasickness; it was a deep and simple pain. No mania could control it. No drug could transform it. And it hurt like hell.

"Tell me a story," I asked him, and he did.

21

What I recount here is what I am able to based on the words that I thought I heard from the man's mouth. I owe it to Tongue for attempting to tell the story that he keeps trapped inside of him. Of course, my transcription will surely fail for the simple fact that language itself has always failed Tongue, or rather his inability to wrap his lips around words always meant that his only true means of expression would be action. Of course, he was more than able to rock the French, so perhaps it was my own ineptitude and not his that always seemed to pose a challenge between us. So if I'm embellishing here or inventing, it's because I knew him mostly by his actions, which had always been pure, whereas his words would forever remain garbled, impeded by the glorious fleshy muscle in his mouth.

The story of Tongue, as recounted in slobbers on the night before I abandoned him on the fishing vessel *The More or Less*, goes as follows:

His name was not Tongue or Billy. His name was Constantine Bloop-Nikolovski. He was born in a small village in the former Yugoslavia amid the upheaval of the crisis in the late eighties that led to the Bosnian War. His father was a rebel soldier, and his mother had been a singer when she was young, mostly performing in coffee houses in Zagreb.

Constantine had been born two months past his due date. When he was finally freed from his mother's womb, the baby was larger than most toddlers, weighing in at fifty-five and a half pounds. His parents attempted to leave their village before the baby was born and firmly believed that the baby's reluctant arrival was a sign of good faith from God, a means for them to buy more time as they waited, ever impatiently, for the arrival of their Canadian visas in the mail. But time finally ran out. Baby Constantine was ready to come out, and he did so a day before his village was bombed. As if that act of fate wasn't cruel enough, it was later discovered that the visas had in fact been delivered to the local post office the day before Constantine's birth, but a roadblock had been set up that made it impossible for Misha, the letter carrier, to pass through on his orange bicycle.

Constantine was born with a normal-sized tongue, or so it seemed. It had been balled up inside the baby's mouth at birth and was attached to his lower frenulum. What was most striking about the child, beyond his size, which was explained away by the fact that he had grown so much in the womb—a whole eleven-month gestation period—was that he never once cried. At first, the midwives believed that this was a bad omen. That he wasn't getting any air. That he wasn't breathing. But the baby was pink and healthy all over and showed all the signs that he was breathing quite well. Constantine's mother knew the truth of her baby's silence. She knew he was keeping quiet so as to keep the household safe from the vigilance of the enemy troops marching through the square. This deep appreciation for the child created an instant bond between mother and son. A remarkable thing when you consider the fact that she'd given birth to an oversized watermelon.

Constantine spent the next twenty-four hours surrounded by his large extended family in utter silence. The entire group had braved the roadblocks, the consequences of breaking curfew, and their collective sense of impending doom in order to celebrate the birth of this hulking miracle child. There was food and there was wine, but no one dared make a sound. Not so much as a peep or a bloop. Such was the reality of a village on the brink of destruction. Constantine represented hope for the family. He was the embodiment of their strength and perseverance, and their joy, albeit silent, couldn't be crushed.

The entire family died the next morning, as did most of the families in the village. And on the second day of his life, Constantine found himself orphaned in the middle of a bombed-out horror show. His extraordinary tongue was discovered by a Canadian Red Cross worker in a hospital a few miles from where'd he'd been found. He was already a legend by the time he arrived at the medical camp as the infant who had survived the shelling without a scratch. But the baby remained tight-lipped. His silence was first attributed to deafness, or shock, and it wasn't until closer inspection of his mouth that the truth was discovered. His attached tongue, rolled up like a piece of rubber hose, was impeding any sound from being emitted from his tiny, powerful body. The doctors snipped his frenulum, and Constantine's tongue unravelled like a wet, pink coil. The Red Cross workers were amazed. It extended three full inches out of the baby's mouth.

Free at last, the child began to bellow louder than any sound of warfare in the vicinity. The tongue quivered in the air as the child protested, in triumphant elephant-like blasts, all the carnage and mania that his first forty-eight hours of being on earth had shown him. He blubbered and wailed as if giving sound to all the pain in all the world.

Constantine cried all night, all week, all month. His tongue refused to stop. He wailed for the duration of the trip to Canada. He bawled through customs and immigration. He howled in the orphanage in Toronto. He cried in his sleep. Cried when he ate. Baby Constantine cried whenever adopting parents came to visit the orphanage. He was rocked, kissed, changed, patted, burped, sung to, pleaded with, and begged to stop. It wasn't long before the nurses began to secretly resent the baby, torn between their compassion and frustration. Nobody could get him to stop crying. Beyond that, no doctor could properly deduce what ailed him.

Although he had been born developed well beyond an ordinary infant, Constantine did not grow at all in those first months of his life. His fontanel didn't close. He remained uncoordinated like a newborn, a screaming lump of life. But as suddenly as the blubbering began, on the anniversary of the day he'd been found, exactly one day after his first birthday, Constantine stopped crying. The baby had mourned the loss of his family for 365 days in a constant, resounding sob. But from that day forward, no more tears were shed. The effect of the year-long vigil meant that his tongue, which had been a remarkable thing to begin with, was now even more impressive and powerful.

After that day, baby Constantine Bloop was happy. He began to grow quickly, and by his second birthday he weighed 105 pounds and stood three feet tall. News of the screaming war child had given him a fair bit of attention in the press. He was already somewhat notorious, but he became even more so with the latest growth spurt. And although at first it didn't seem that anyone would ever adopt such a colicky nightmare, his new charming demeanour and record-breaking stature made him a first-round choice for all kinds of hopeful adopting parents.

Constantine bounced around the country from

Victoria, BC, to the Yukon to Montreal, Quebec, sharing homes of all different sorts of families in different kinds of dwellings. In those early years, he learned how to kayak, how to speak French, how to chop wood, how to snowshoe, how to ice skate, how to fish, how to wrestle, how to sing, how to make an igloo—all by the time he was five years old.

After an extensive review process by the orphanage, it looked as though Constantine would finally get a permanent home with a real surrogate mother and father of his own. Their names were Lily and Henry Grace. They were a wealthy couple who had followed Constantine's unfortunate story as news columnists abroad. They themselves had spent time in Sarajevo during the war. If he had been adopted by the Graces, Constantine would have, no doubt, lived a charmed life between Lily and Henry's house in the Beaches of Toronto, Ontario, and their two-acre cottage in the Muskokas. Besides that, they were good people who, knowing first-hand what atrocities took place in the war, wanted to shower the baby with unwavering love in an attempt to reset the balance of justice in the universe.

However, on the day the Graces were set to take Constantine, fate once again stepped in. Objuck and Olega came on the scene. They presented themselves as Constantine's relatives. The sole surviving members of the Bloop-Nikolovski family. As you know, they ran an ice cream parlour in Oshawa, Ontario, and, as you also know, they were nuts, but they were able to prove their place of origin and a blood link to the child on Objuck's side—apparently, as the illegitimate half-brother of Constantine's paternal grandfather's first wife.

And so Constantine was sent to live with the proprietors of the ice cream parlour instead. What had been a mythical start for the boy had been reduced to common living. Constantine was too big and too special to grow properly in such a cold, dreary place. He never fit. From the constant teasing he received in the schoolyard to the mediocrity of the day-to-day routine of the parlour, it was obvious that he was meant for greater things. Still, Constantine never rebelled. He always did what he was told. He developed his own rituals and interests from his early years: singing, wrestling, food. He loved watching wrestling. He had an appetite for all things—and the duller and more predictable life became around him, the greater his appetite grew.

I'd like to believe that leaving Tongue on that fishing boat, and getting him away from my own certain doom, was the greatest gift I could have given him. I want to believe this, but I can't be sure. To help ease my conscience, the next morning, before Les gave me directions on how to meet up with his cousin after we docked, I slipped Tongue the cigar box filled with about half of the money from my father. He was still sleeping when I stuffed it inside his duffle bag. It was his share for taking me this far. I hoped that if his indomitable spirit couldn't keep him afloat (although I knew it would), the dough would help. Was I buying him off? Appeasing my guilt for abandoning him? Yes. But it was the least I could do to say thank you to Constantine, the miraculous war child with the giant tongue.

22

On land again, my inheritance significantly depleted, separated from the mysterious creature who'd helped me escape the confines of a life I never wanted, and navigating surprisingly well in Henrietta rolling though the city of fog, I was lucid and determined to find my mother now. But along with that kind of clarity came certain stark realizations of what had occurred over the past three weeks: my father's death, my attempted rebirth, my escape, the near misses on the Trans-Canada, a botched history dredged up and spat out, and, of course, the flash of that blade.

Had I really killed a man? Or had I merely injured him? Either way, had I conjured up my father in those grotesque moments in the back of the limo with Jack and hacked him to pieces? If it were true, then my father would have his final laugh beyond the grave. It would be only a matter of days, weeks maybe, before they found me, spotted Henrietta. Identified Tongue. We stuck out badly. It'd be easy to pin it on us. This would be the failure that had loomed over me since setting out. How quickly I had stepped out of one muck heap and landed in another. This time, more vast, more based on hard facts. And in this real-time conviction, I was the new terror. I'd become the very thing that had pursued me. I'd become my father. After all, I was driving the dead man's car. It didn't matter that he was gone. He lived on inside me. And for the first time, I considered myself no better than the lousy drunk.

By the time I reached Lancaster Avenue, I had convinced myself of how it would end. There'd be no time to deliver the news to Mom. There'd be no answers about my lost child. They'd find Tongue first, and they'd put pressure on him to give me up, turn me in. But he wouldn't budge. He'd sacrifice himself for me, hold his glorious tongue and take the fall. After all, it was his knife. Even if I buried Henrietta at the bottom of the ocean, shaved my head, changed my name, he was impossible to disguise. I was certain that I was being followed anyway. Talk about sticking out: The long white car crept along the harbour streets like some big white shark. And the crazy woman with the baby bangs and the crawling skin. What was her name? Call her Winnie. Call her Big Ben's girl. She was the guilty one. This paranoia mounted, and by the time I was in front of the boarded-up asylum, I was ready to make a run for it, even though I was so close.

Shep stood smoking a cigarette by a dumpster. I knew it was him even before he introduced himself to me because he was the spitting image of his weather-beaten cousin, Lester. The only difference was that he was decades older and walked with a limp. But just as tiny and grey. Also, Shep, unlike the hen-pecked Les, beamed when he saw me step out of the limo. Bared a toothless smile and hobbled towards me. We shook hands and went around to the delivery entrance. I wasn't sure what Mor and Les had told him. He didn't seem to care why I wanted to look inside the hospital, and I was glad that he didn't ask any questions.

Shep pulled out a ring of rusted keys and started to test them on the lock of the imposing double doors. The place had gone to the weeds. Every window had been boarded up with wood that showcased the work of teenage graffiti artists: various spray-painted renditions of the F-word and outrageously proportioned sex parts. I distinctly read the word WACKO in dripping red paint. The real-life image of that structure in front of me didn't match the haunting one of soft lime green I'd kept in my mind all of those years. In the flesh, it looked the way I wanted it to look. As if somehow my feelings about the hospital had actually altered its physical architecture. Now I was able to trade in my fantastical mental arrangements for decaying grey concrete.

Though the gracious geezer already had one club foot in the grave, Shep's hands moved at lightning speed. There was still some life in him yet. He rang out curses under his breath as he tried to jam each key into the corroded keyhole without any luck. "Sonofacockbitingitchybitch!"

Finally, a key turned, and Shep let out a gasp of relief, flashing toothless and exasperated. But much to his chagrin, the door still wouldn't budge. More cursing, the likes of which I'd never quite heard before: "Fek. Fek. Fek the world on Sundee morn. Fek me eyes. Fek me soul. Fek me burning red arsehole."

Shep leaned against the door with all of his might and strained to make the thing move. I thought he'd surely launch his bowels loose. Then, to my surprise and delight, he started to kick the door. The sound was bare bone against bare wood. The impact sent him reeling backwards in pain, hopping on his peg leg and spraying the world with words that sounded like: *piss, Grolsch, relish, riptide, Jesus, Mary,* and *Joseph.*

I thought that some of the crazy must have rubbed off on him after all those years of working inside. But I soon realized that this wasn't the case. Shep was failing to accomplish even the simplest of tasks, when at one time he would have been in charge of the upkeep of the entire joint, inside and out. This lapse into fury must have been brought on by revisiting a place that had been reduced to ruins after he'd spent so long caring for it and grooming it. It must have been hard for him to encounter it that way. The same way he found himself now: defunct, useless, waiting to be torn down. That's why he wouldn't give up. He collected himself on the ground surrounded by overgrown grass and contemplated his next heroic move. How to get inside the bloody door?

"Let's ram it," I said.

"What are you saying?"

"Let's bash our way inside."

And before Shep could try to stop me, I was already back behind the wheel of the limousine. The engine was already running, and I started to bulldoze my way inside. Henrietta held up well. I had finally discovered her true purpose as I continued to smash and smash into the side of the decaying building: put the car into reverse, back up, and accelerate again. The sound of tires in mud and the clanking of metal bumper against concrete was the sound of reckless freedom. It was a symbolic prison break for all of the past inmates who'd lived locked inside. It was my mother's work, and in doing it, I was wrecking my father's pride and joy: Henrietta. Breaking into that mental institution would be her greatest mission.

I hit my head in the process, and a small mouse began to grow above my eye. It was hard to see past the dust and debris that had been lifted from my assault. I couldn't get a real glimpse down the checkerboard halls. The car, apart from being crumpled, was stuck inside the entranceway. Her front end slipped about four feet inside the hospital's common room, while her ass end protruded out in the sunlight, her back tires still spinning. I climbed out of the moon roof and down the rear window. When the dust settled, I saw the place as a grey desiccated skull. The limo, a large white tongue stuck out at the world.

Shep stood fixed about twenty feet away. He was

chewing on his nails, biting them and spitting them out like sunflower seeds. The man was twitching too as he took in the sudden calm rising from the demo. When he saw me, he threw his arms up in the air and waved them around frantically, conducting his bitter laughter.

"Wait till I tell Doc Hartley. Wait till I tell him. Jesus!"

Doc Hartley, Shep would later explain, was the man responsible for both the one-time success and the eventual shut down of the hospital. A brilliant doctor according to the aging former head custodian. But some say a quack with bogus therapies. I knew right away that I'd need to pay the good doctor a visit, but I'll get to that later.

Shep and I squeezed our way past Henrietta and walked inside that dust-filled hospital. I didn't know what I was hoping to discover entering the cracked skull. Her room? Her bed? A chair where she'd sat for supper? A bathtub where she'd washed her body? An old television set? A cup she'd drunk from? A pillow where she'd laid her head? A line on the ceiling that went sideways in a zigzag that she'd find herself staring up at while daydreaming? Her fork? Her spoon? The craft table where she'd spent afternoons making doilies? Doilies? The massive clock on the wall? Those steps? Florescent light bulbs? A pillbox? What stories lay behind all of these nameless artifacts?

I could have rejected them all if I'd wanted to. Seen them as nothing more than dead, rotting, forgotten objects. But they were all I had of her, so I had no choice but to accept them as being imbued with even an ounce of life. I wanted to touch everything, run my fingers across everything the way the blind read bumps or features on a face. I thought that I'd somehow recognize her in recognizing the materials in my hands. But really I found nothing more in them than dust and a reminder of their function. A toothbrush was a toothbrush. A toilet was a toilet. A sink was a sink. These were the things that humans used. All shaped in reference to the human body. A book held with two hands, its pages flipped by the index finger and thumb. A gown drapes over the shoulders and down the back. Slippers cover ankles and feet. Windows designed to be looked through at eye level. Beds the length of a torso, raised two feet in the air. Combs spread strands of hair on the head. Glasses sit on the bridge of the nose and over the ears. A table. A room. A hallway. Larger rooms. Smaller rooms. Doorways wide enough to enter and exit. A floor stretched out to accommodate the movement of people.

It was all evidence of men and women who had touched, shat, slept, eaten, bathed, sat, walked, fallen, slopped, pissed, vomited, bled. But nothing remained of the stories that had brought them here, or the stories that had played out inside the walls of the sanatorium itself. Situational dramas. Divine comedies. All that remained was the perfunctory extensions of people reduced to their bare essentials—walking slabs—doped up, sterilized, shaved, and kept dry. Void of identity, void of any emotional history, hope, or desire. It's what I imagined the end of the world looking like.

Before walking out of that place forever, I read the following phrase on Doc Hartley's office door:

> To Believe in a New Future,
> You Must Believe in a New Past,
> Invented and Perfected in the Present.

Of course, the esoteric motto was hard to make out at first, as someone had spray-painted a large magenta phallus over it, but I could still decipher the words. It was different from the generic feel-good jargon you pick up on the sides of buses advertising real estate, and it was more convoluted than the pop psychology you encounter on afternoon talk-therapy shows. I could have just ignored it, or taken it as self-help blather, but there was something in it that intrigued me.

Was this the philosophy that had been propagated in the hospital when my mother was an inmate? If so, what did it really mean? To believe in the future suggested hope. I got that. It made sense to me. But what did it mean to believe in a new past? What other past could one believe in? Was this Hartley pushing time travel? Moreover, it was the insistence on inventing the past in the present that made my brain start to hurt. If you invented your past in the present in order to believe in the future, wouldn't your future just be the past invention of a present spent inventing, not living? Yes, it made me feel dumb. I can only imagine how those words affected the poor slobs who had inhabited those halls. Had they ever been able to believe in their futures or their pasts? How exactly had they perfected their beliefs anyway? Could they have predicted the futures of the place? I wished for their sake that they could see it now in its perfected crumbling future state.

It wasn't hard to understand why it'd been closed down. My personal feelings and mania aside, it was cramped, damp, and stultifying. Even if I was making way more out of Hartley's motto than what was really there, I wanted to tear it all down. It was a real past for me, encountered in the present. Although I'd done my best to obliterate it in my mind for years, I was now standing in it. I was at the centre of it. The image of the bars on the infirmary doors would forever stay etched in my mind.

23

Old Shep sat in back. He had agreed to be my guide for the next part of my search. It'd taken us a good deal of rocking and shoving Henrietta back and forth to get her out of the busted-up mouth of the asylum. Between taking his directions over my shoulder, which were sending us further east, I grilled him in an attempt to learn more about my mother's therapist. Was he even a therapist? How old was the man? What made his therapies so controversial? Why had they shut down his practice? Where were we going?

Shep had grown suspicious of me ever since I crashed my limo into the side of the boarded-up building. Fair enough. He wasn't really telling me what I wanted to know. Maybe he thought I should be committed myself. Is that where we were going? Was Shep one of Doc Hartley's henchmen commissioned to go out and bring back freshly battered brains to lobotomize? Shep assured me that all my questions would be answered when I met the man in the flesh. He was certain the doctor would be willing to speak with me. We made a quick stop at a roadside donair shop in Moncton so that Shep could pee. He said his prostate was shot to hell. It was then that he did his best to fill me in on more details about Hartley.

"They welcome all kinds down on the farm."

"The farm?"

We were heading to Doc Hartley's potato farm in Prince Edward Island.

"Quite the place, I've heard," he said. "Doing more than harvesting spud, I bet."

According to Shep, Doc Hartley disappeared for a few years after the hospital in Saint John had been closed down. His medical license had been taken away, and the chatter around the harbour was that he himself had cracked up, although no legal suits had been filed against him, and no one could find a soul to speak a bad word against him.

"I tell ya, he's a good man. Some people in this world have imaginations that's so big that they step on other peoples toes."

Shep had only recently re-established contact with the doctor, who had called him one day out of the blue to ask if he wanted a job on his new farm. He didn't say it was a hospital exactly. He called it a sanctuary. Shep said that he turned down the job because he didn't want to get caught up in any kind of scandal. Although he respected the man, Shep seemed a bit wary about this new project of Hartley's.

"To be honest," Shep said, "I don't exactly know

where we're headed. I never been to the place myself. Curious more than anything."

As we continued our journey, I pictured an endless field with patients dressed as farmers, hundreds of them, bent doubled at the waist, digging through the dirt, unearthing large black potatoes. The image of it haunted me for the remainder of our drive, and as we made our way towards the terrifying thirteen-kilometre Confederation Bridge that connects New Brunswick to PEI, I felt sick to my stomach.

The road was miraculously suspended above the ocean. It stretched out towards an unseen future. Literally. I couldn't see where the thing ended. It was two lanes of traffic going both ways. I held my breath as we approached. One wrong turn of the wheel, and we'd be over the edge—a 130-foot drop into oblivion. I started to panic. By the time we reached the halfway point, I could no longer see land in any direction. Not where we'd come from or where we were going. It was only water. Only overcast skies and water. I tried to focus intently on the narrow road before us and to block out all other angles. It didn't help that the truck in front of us carrying farm equipment was going so slowly. The voyage was taking forever. What if we broke down or ran out of gas? There was no way of turning around, no turning back. We could only go straight—inch by treacherous inch—moving ever closer to the island of buried potatoes.

There are moments in life when the clouds part

unexpectedly and the light shines brighter than a million suns. It's what we addicts call an epiphany, a rushing in of awareness, a deep revelation and recollection. Finding myself inside that beat-up old limousine suspended in the air over the Northumberland Strait, completely stricken by fear, with only one thought on my mind—what the fuck is happening?—I had my very first epiphany.

It came in the form of a matted squirrel's tail. Shep found the thing on the floor of the backseat, and when he held it up to me and asked what it was, I nearly swerved us to our deaths. It was about fourteen inches long in a sick combination of purple and copper. I thought it was a bloated dead rat or some other rodent I'd picked up along my trek though the endless fields and forests of Canada, but it wasn't. Bound together at one end by a red rubber band was Jack's long, disgusting, greasy ponytail. Frayed at the bottom and jaggedly hacked off at the top. The work had been anything but precise, but it didn't matter. The sheer joy and relief in knowing exactly what piece of the man I'd taken that night at the carnival was truly overwhelming. I instantly remembered the act and how it truly had transpired. The wrestling match, his hot breath, my difficulty in opening up the Swiss Army knife, and then the glorious detachment of that goddamn mane. It was better than castration, for I'd managed to remove a vestige of the man without drawing blood or implicating myself.

I held the ponytail up, and in an instant my mounting fears of being caught up in a B-movie plot were dispelled. Jackass had nothing on me except for a bad haircut. And yet, holding that limp thing in my hand, I knew that I'd taken away all his power. I rolled down the window and tossed it over the bridge. Shep didn't know what to make of any of it.

Then, almost by some miracle, the island began to come slowly into focus. It was just a red line on the horizon at first, which I glimpsed through my teary eyes. But soon it began to spread out as we got closer. It was like seeing a photograph take shape out of nothingness; a picture appeared as we neared those red sandy shores. I saw it rise out from underneath the currents below as solid earth—real earth dredged up in all its glory. For surely this was the most beautiful place on the planet. The sun came out. We had only about another kilometre to go, but I was getting impatient, and no longer for fear of being airborne—it was this burning desire to touch down on that land that was making me want to scream. I was actually giddy.

By the time we finally made it safely across, Shep had to pee again, so we pulled over at the first stretch of gift shops and tourists booths. We weren't far from a welcome sign where you could stick your head inside a lobster cut-out and get your picture taken. As my guide wandered off to relieve himself, I got out of the car and took in the sudden silence of being on an island. There were so few people around. If you were looking for a spot to be alone, this was the place. I was far enough away from my shitty factory town now to forget. I was sufficiently marooned now to start over again. But, of course, I hadn't come here to forget but to remember. Would I be able to recognize her face?

When Shep got back, we continued our trek through the red rolling hills of PEI. The land was fertile and rich. Everywhere were farms and waterfronts, farmers and fishermen living off the land. It was hard to believe that it was considered a province. It was so small. Every five minutes or so, we passed through another little town. The red soil and the deep-green grass and the yellow sun and the blue-green waters were all so vivid. Almost make-believe. There was something old-fashioned about it all too. As if I had stepped into the past. Not because of any overt signs of another era but because of the simplicity of the atmosphere. It was how I imagined the world was before humans soiled it with toxins. The island was pure.

I'd been forced to encounter nature for my entire journey, but this was the first time that nature actually opened up for me, and I felt as though I could breathe. Perhaps it was just the weight that lifted after Shep's discovery in the back seat. Maybe it was facing those fears in the asylum and realizing the sky wouldn't fall after all. Quite the opposite, in fact—as I looked across the Cavendish harbour, I no longer saw a ceiling caving in on me; I saw the earth in relation to the water, and the water in relation to the sky, and myself there in relation to it all.

24

Hartley saw us separately. Shep and I had shown ourselves in when we first arrived at the colossal colonial farmhouse. The acreage was set well back from the red dirt road. Potato fields spread out in all directions. There was a big red barn, twice as big as the house at the far end of the property. I was getting nervous sitting in the front room by myself. I didn't know if it'd be better if I took something to combat my anxiety or if I should go in to see the man raw. I wanted to have my wits intact. The problem was that I'd become accustomed to needing chemicals in my veins to function properly. I couldn't trust the mood swings. I decided to take half a pill to hedge my bets.

Shep had been in Hartley's office for about an hour. The wait wasn't helping my condition. I started to wonder if maybe I had misjudged this lead. There wasn't a soul in sight. The entranceway, all that I'd seen of it anyway, was clean, not too fancy, impersonal. There were comfortable sofas and armchairs, a fireplace that seemed to actually work, some rosewood tables, and a grandfather clock. The clock also seemed to work. I'd been glancing up at the swinging arm throughout my wait. A large bay window opened up onto the land to a full view of the big barn. There were no animals anywhere. I started to breathe deeply.

I didn't want to allow myself to get carried away in there with Hartley. I knew I couldn't give him the full inventory of events—it'd make me sound crazy—but I also knew that I had to give him a certain number of the facts if I wanted to walk away with anything from the man. I hoped that Shep wouldn't embellish what had happened back at the hospital. Hartley would already have the advantage in our conversations if he'd been given an account of the destruction I was capable of doing. The more I thought this way, the more I began to doubt myself and to consider how I must come across to others. How would Hartley see me? Usually, I couldn't care less. People are going to think what they're going to think. If I spent my life worrying about appearances, I'd never go outside. But this meeting with Hartley was different. I needed him to trust me, or at least to hear me out, because I wanted something from him. An address, an oral history, a photograph—something.

It's awful to be beholden to others like that. Awful to have to kneel down before those who have something on you. I'd been staying clear of those types of relationships and entanglements my whole life. It's why I could never hold down a job for more than a few months. Why I never finished school, never owned a phone, never opened a bank account. I refuse to sign contracts or to participate in the mass delusion that society is under. A big sham. I've always believed in opting out well before being ensnared. Because I knew better, I did better. It usually boiled down to needing cash anyway. That's what most transactions in this life are about. As if that's the only need in the world. Waiting impatiently in the front room like a beggar wanting some coins or a rookie wanting to be called up to the big league, I wanted something from the man behind the closed door, and I resented the intrinsic power he held over me.

My gut began to cramp, worse than usual. It presented a new, more pressing need: a toilet. I considered barging in on Shep and Hartley's reunion. What were they doing in there anyway? But I thought the better of it. Not the best form of introduction—a frantic woman demanding to use the bathroom. I took it upon myself to find one on my own, although this was risky too. I didn't want to be introduced to Hartley as a snoop either. But my bowels solved the dilemma for me; they told me what to do. And after trying a few locked doors down the long, sun-filled corridor, I found the john and did what my body instructed.

I couldn't have been in there very long, but by the time I got back to my unpleasant perch in the waiting room, the door to Hartley's office was open and the men were gone. I peeked inside but found no one. It was a cruel joke to play on someone in my position. I'd been waiting for him patiently. I was disoriented enough. Now I began to consider the possibility that I was becoming completely delusional. Where was I? What in God's name was I doing there?

Without a soul in sight to confirm or deny any speculation that I was descending into delusion, I tried to stick to the facts of the matter. But only having been recently introduced to my immediate surroundings, it was hard for me to even confirm what I thought I knew. The clock, the sofa, the fireplace—they were where I'd left them. I returned to the bathroom down the hall. It was still there; the toilet still hummed from my flush. I went back to the entranceway, drew back the curtain. The barn, the fields, the rows and rows of potatoes—I'd already inventoried these things and was relieved to find them where I'd left them, but still no sign of Shep or Hartley. And where was Henrietta? I'd parked the car sideways on the grass, the front facing the silo. I remember doing this in case I wanted to bolt, make a quick getaway. The long red dirt path leading from the road to the farm was narrow. I remember thinking that in order to get out of there, I'd have to back up about fifty feet, or wind up making a U-turn into the potato fields, unless I parked it sideways facing the silo. That's why I did it. I remember doing it—I was thinking ahead. So the only changes since going into the bathroom were that Hartley's office door was open, Shep and the doctor had vanished, and the car was gone. The logical conclusion was that Shep and Hartley had taken off in the limo. I clung to this reasoning for fear of the alternative: that I was losing it.

I felt around for my keys. The hawk! The keychain was in my pocket. I pulled it out and jangled it in front of my face. I could hear it and see it. So they couldn't have taken the car. This destroyed my theory of what had happened to the men, but at least it proved that the car was real. Digging deeper in my pockets, I found the baby picture of my son. The picture was real, but it didn't mean that the child was real. Is being lost as good as being gone? Or never existing?

I ran out the front door, sufficiently bugged. To my relief, I found Henrietta. It should have instantly dispelled my fears, but there was still the issue of where it was parked. Had someone moved it? I had parked it on a sideways angle, or so I thought. But without any trace of tire marks in the red dirt to confirm this, it meant I hadn't. There's a difference between wanting to do something and actually doing it. I guess I had wanted to park sideways, facing the silo, and so I'd remembered doing it that way. In thinking it, I'd done it. But, of course, I hadn't. The car wasn't sideways, wasn't facing the silo. It was straight and facing the porch. Yes, I was bugged, spooked too. I figured I'd entered the funny farm and the place was rubbing off on me.

I sat on a large porch swing and lit a cigarette. The movement of the swing and the nicotine calmed me down. The seat made a steady creaking sound as I rocked, which was not unpleasant, but much like the grandfather clock—hypnotic. I flicked away cigarette ashes and stared off into those potato fields. Far off in the distance, the double barn doors swung open. That's when I saw Hartley's women.

They came out en masse, huddled together in a group at first, but soon they began to spread out across the fields. They were dressed uniformly in blue A-line dresses with white polka dots. About fifty of them with matching hairdos: sharp A-line bobs with short blunt bangs. They carried books of various sizes and colours— not hardbound published books; they were notebooks. As the women began to disperse across the farm, I could see that they were reading from these notebooks. Looking intently at the pages and soundlessly mouthing the words that stared back at them off the page. Some found trees to sit under; others set themselves up cross-legged by the creek; some plunked themselves down right in the middle of the potatoes.

I knew they were reading different things because of how they were all reacting differently to what they read. Some were lost in the pages; others scanned them intently; some were smiling; others were wide-eyed. I was awestruck watching them lick their fingers and turn those pages. There was no break in their concentration either. These women were all focused with an eerie ferocity to the page. I was spellbound by these women as I tried to read their movements and motivations, silently in the pasture.

I must have sat there watching for about an hour. The entire time, not one of them looked up from her notebook or uttered a single word out loud. I wanted to scream at them, clap my hands, do something to break this spell. If I could get them to look up at me, it would mean that they were real, but if I pinched myself, woke myself up (if that's what was going on), and they were to disappear, I'd know that they never existed in the first place.

As if willing it, a sound did begin to rise that cut through the ghastly silence. It was a tractor that buzzed and sputtered and echoed out across the land. I jolted back from the intrusion of noise. The women remained, and remained fixed to their reading.

Shep bounced his way towards me, sitting high up on the big-wheeled contraption, which continued to roar. The ancient little man looked like a quivering bird hunched on his seat. He said something to me that I couldn't hear over the snarl of the engine. He shut the thing off and squinted down at me.

"Eh?" he said.

When I didn't respond, he repeated the question. "You been in to talk to the doc yet?"

I marvelled at his complicity regarding the messed-up library that had sprouted on the farm. "What the hell are you doing?"

"Cutting the lawn."

"When did this happen? I've been waiting for hours."

"Just now. Hartley's a persuasive man. Says it's been tough looking after the place all by himself. Wouldn't take no for an answer. Got my old job back."

His cavalier attitude was pissing me off. I couldn't connect the events of the past few hours. I said nothing. I thought it was better than raging at him, but I was furious. To have been handed off, seemingly forgotten about.

When I didn't say anything, Shep said, "You oughta go in and talk to the doctor."

Then he tried to start the tractor back up. It coughed a few times before catching. He rode away bouncing. I sat back down on the swing. At least Shep existed. However inane, he was real.

I contemplated going out and trying to engage with the women. To try talking to them. They were all different ages, shapes, and backgrounds. Yet, because of the symmetry of their clothes and hair and actions, I saw them as one group, one entity. I wanted to address them as one. I wished I had a loudspeaker to call out to them, but I doubt I could have taken them away from their books. Who were these women? What were they reading? What could possibly attract them with such magnetism?

The startling thought that one of them could be my mother paralyzed me. Which one was she? I began to regard them differently with this line of thinking. Could I really be that close to her? What would I say to her? It would be impossible to pick her out of that crowd. Really, any one of them could have been the one who had given birth to me. If I had been more reasonable at the time, and I couldn't have been, I could have begun to isolate them based on factors such as age and hair colour. But it would still have been guesswork. They were all potential mothers out there reading soundlessly without a regard for another living creature.

The front door swung open, and Doc Hartley stepped outside. Our eyes met. He didn't look away, and neither did I. His beard was what struck me first. It was big and bushy and orange and wiry. After the beard, I analyzed his red cheeks. They were rosy and fat and bulging. His nose was broad. Then I scanned his body. Hidden underneath an impeccably white lab coat were a buxom chest, full waist, and heavy legs. He was wearing overalls. He was old. I don't know why I expected him to be younger. That said, he carried himself with a vitality that suggested youth. He wasn't bent or hunched but rather open. His shoulders were back. His big round gut looked firm. There were wrinkles around his deep-blue eyes—red flaps of skin all around his eyes. It was the wrinkles that aged him, as well as his large ears, also the tufts of nose hairs protruding.

Doc Hartley was humming under his breath. Then he started to giggle. He extended a meaty hand to me and said, "Oh, there you are."

He exclaimed this as if he'd been searching for me. As if I hadn't been waiting on his doorstep for hours, left to rot on his porch. He repeated this phrase, pleased that he found me, and planted himself down beside me on the swing. The thing jolted with the added weight of his body. We shook hands, and he started to swing us vigorously. I rocked in time with the mad rhythm of the man.

"What are they doing?" I asked him.

"Hmm?"

"The women."

"Oh, them. Well, isn't it obvious? They're reading."

"What are they reading?"

"Their stories, of course."

25

You've come a long way.

Shep told you?

Bits and pieces. He said you left the place in ruins.

Not quite. It was pretty rough when I found it. I just wanted to get inside the door.

What did you find?

Nothing. There was nothing left but junk. It's a junkyard now.

Yes, they'll tear it down soon.

I'm glad I got to see it before it vanished completely.

What were you hoping to find?

I just wanted to find the hospital itself. I had a vague picture of it in my head.

You'd been there before?

Once when I was a kid.

What was it like going back?

Awful.

Is that why you smashed it?

No. I wanted to get inside the door.

Did you hurt yourself?

I bumped my head, and it bled a little.

And the car?

It still runs. It's a piece of shit anyway.

Odd choice of vehicle, a limo. You don't see many people driving limos.

I didn't choose it. It was given to me by my father. He left it to me in his will.

That was kind of him.

I don't see it that way. He was not a kind man.

What kind of man was he?

A tyrant-pig.

Do you believe a man can change? Perhaps it was a peace offering.

Nope. It was a piece of shit. A setup. He'd hidden things in the glovebox.

Really? Like what?

Money. Thousands.

An inheritance.

Nope. There was a picture inside the box with the money.

Can you describe the picture?

A picture of a baby boy.

Anything else you can tell me about the baby boy?

His name was Billy. He was my son. He died.

The picture brought up unpleasant feelings?

What do you think?

Is that what you meant by setup? Setting you up to suffer?

Always. I don't want to talk about him anymore.
Are you referring to Billy or your father?
Both.

※

How do you find the island?
It's beautiful.
I'm glad. And this place?
Strange. There's no denying it's strange.
You're just not used to it. Where is home?
Somewhere in Southern Ontario. It's not important. It could be anywhere. I'm just glad to be away from it. Although it still doesn't feel far enough away. I just recently escaped.

In the limo with the money and the picture of Billy?
Exactly.
When was this?
I can't be certain.
And that doesn't concern you?
No. It started with my father's funeral. I left the day they put him in the ground.

Did you have an idea of where you were going?
I wanted to find the hospital.
Was that your first impulse?
My first thought was to leave.
Why that hospital? Why did you set that place as the end point of your journey? There are many hospitals between Southern Ontario and Saint John, New

Brunswick. Hospitals that aren't boarded up.

I was looking for my mother. We left her in the hospital in Saint John.

What were you hoping to say to her when you found her?

I don't know. That he was dead. I thought it would do her some good to know.

You blame your father for her ending up in the hospital?

I blame my father for everything.

So that's why you found me? That's why you're here?

Yes. Do you think you would remember her?

Maybe. I've treated thousands of patients. I'd need something to go on.

Like what? A date? A name? Her name was Winifred McKeagan.

Okay. I will start there. But there's another problem. It concerns the work I did at the hospital in Saint John and the work I do here at the farm.

Does it have something to do with why they shut you down?

It has everything to do with that. The medical community has become obsessed with pills. That's become the current and, really, only form of treatment. Drugs. Altering one's mind to balance the chemistry in the brain.

I know all about it. I'm an addict. I've been self-medicating for years.

And how has that worked for you?

- 207 -

It hasn't. It's awful. I swear to God it's crippled me.

I admire your honesty. We can get you clean if you're willing. Everyone in the world is addicted to something.

I would be willing to get clean, but I've given up on the idea that it will ever happen.

It will happen. I have a cure for addiction. The work we do here has been shown to produce marvellous results.

And you don't use pills?

Never. The human body and mind have more power and can create more sensation than the effects of any drug in science.

But what about the women in the field? They look like goddamn zombies. They're not on drugs?

Never. Do you think they would be able to concentrate on their work if they were on drugs? They may look like zombies, but I can assure you they're anything but. They're working hard.

On what?

The work we do here involves telling stories. I discovered some time ago in my practice that one's suffering is directly related to the stories that we tell ourselves. You've just laid out for me tiny pieces of a story. The objects are all props in the drama of your memory. And that memory has caused you to suffer. Would you agree with that?

Yes.

What would happen if you rewrote the story? I'm

not talking about denial. That's what happens when we suppress the story or try to bury it. What if you were to write a story so fantastic, so beautifully recounted and vivid and perfect, and repeated that story to yourself so often and with such vehemence that it became true? It would obliterate your suffering. It would actually take away the pain from the past.

To believe in a new future, you must believe in a new past, invented and perfected in the present.

You've read my work.

I read it on the door to your office in the junkyard.

The key is in the perfecting. You must become a master storyteller for the story to take effect.

That's what the women in the field are doing?

Absolutely. They're perfecting their stories. Each one of them writing and rewriting the names, objects, places, and events of a past too unbearable to exist.

Is my mother in that field?

That would be impossible. The woman who you call your mother, Winifred, even if she is out there, would cease to exist. She would have been rewritten. If she came to me many years ago, I imagine that she has perfected and fulfilled her story by now. She'd be living her rewritten life.

And how would she do that?

With discipline. A strict regimen of writing and reading. That's how you perfect it. Rest assured, she is absolutely free from pain. Those women have negated suffering. For you, it would be easy.

Why would you say that? What do you know about me?

You've already told me everything. I hate to break it to you, but the suffering you carry so blatantly on your face and in your voice isn't new. It's not original.

What the fuck kind of thing is that to say to someone?

It's tough to accept this, I know. But your story, however little I know already, is common. Trite. Quite boring, actually.

I never said it was interesting.

Then why hold onto it? Why continue to bow down to it? You may have put the tyrant-pig in the ground, but he is still very much alive in how he haunts you. Would you deny it?

No. But you have no right to dismiss me. It hurts like hell.

Oh, my dear, no. I want nothing more than for you to find comfort. But it can only start once you accept the banality of your plight. It's meaningless, I assure you. You've been suffering for nothing. No cause, my dear.

How the hell can you say that? Where the fuck do you get off?

Please, lower your voice. I don't mean to upset you. You will come to see how even your voice has failed you. The futility in crying out.

That's only because no one cares to hear.

People hear. Of course they do. People encounter the suffering written over every inch of this world, but they're powerless because they think that there is some profound logic to suffering. There isn't. It's a void. Imagine all those lives spent recounting and retelling such drivel. I've already heard your story. Not from you. Not your specific tale of heartbreak and woe. But from others. Hundreds—no, thousands—of others, and it's always the same. It's this absurd game of dominos, except instead of numbered blocks it's men and women smashing into one another, knocking one another down. That's the real history of humanity. It's my intention to end the game. To build a structure that will withstand the force of those repeated blows, those falling blocks. And I've done it. The medical officials couldn't fathom the simplicity and genius of it, so they shut me down. But I've rebuilt my practice. Here, on the farm. It took me just three years to do it. Here, where you're invited to nullify the past, to reinvent it by telling a new story. I've heard stories so horrible that the teller couldn't possibly imagine rewriting them. But they did, they do. It's because the story was so dull to begin with. Not dull as in lacking in conflict and elaborate brutality—they always have that. I mean dull as in predictable. Let's take you as an example. What do I know about your story? Let's see, we'll start with the obvious. You're angry, furious, beaten down, lost. You're a slave to your addictions. You're haunted by the dead. Your father was a drunk. He too was an addict. Why? Because his father was a drunk. And if he wasn't, he was miserable. Couldn't find work. And if he could, the work didn't satisfy him.

And if it did, it didn't matter because there was never enough money to support his desires. There never is. Talk about fantasy—progress, big salaries, mortgages—this is delusional thinking. These are things void of meaning. Because the man was miserable, he took it out on those around him. His wife. His children. You. And because his wife was trapped, exhausted, unfulfilled, she struggled in all that she did. The outside world had failed her, so she retreated inside her head, but her head was full of addiction too. Booze, yes, but fantasy—escape—progress. She had children or she didn't. She got rid of the baby or she lost it. Or she cared for it, and it grew up and ran away. She began to see the futility of her actions, of all actions. Then one day she found nobility in her suffering. She became selfless, disciplined. She withstood the cruelty around her. But something happened: the family dog died, they lost the house, someone got laid off, someone was unfaithful, a car accident, cancer, drugs, drunk driving, prison, more drugs, not enough money. All drivel. All boring. The woman can't take it. The child is lost. Escape! Pills, a bridge, a rope. Even suicide fails her. And if she is successful, then what? Then the child must make sense of what he finds: his mother hanging in the basement. The child is mortified. Blinded by grief. There is no drug on earth strong enough. The child looks for answers. For someone to blame. Blame the father. Blame the children. Blame the dog. Blame God. It still doesn't work. Blame the world. Hate the world. There's a good idea. Brutalize everyone around you, and the cycle continues. Escape one gravesite to discover another. Endlessly spinning in this predictable freak show. I've heard the story. It's always the same. It never changes. Nothing can mask the unhappiness. It's time to tell a new story.

26

Doc Hartley was a madman. But he was also damn convincing, or maybe he only came across that way because I was too weak to know any better. What was more, most of what he said made sense to me, but I also agreed with him. Underneath his calm exterior, he was inwardly seething. He had absorbed the hours and hours of gut-wrenching accounts of miserable lives, and he recognized despair instantly. He refused to accept it any longer. His own perversity came in the idea that he thought he'd found the cure for human suffering. But I wouldn't understand how misguided he was until much later. At first, I was just hooked. He promised me a way out. I didn't let go of my original intention in seeking him out: I still wanted to find my mother. But after day one of my stay, even I agreed that I had to get clean, that the sickness had gone on far too long. Perhaps I was able to accept this and was so ready to trust him because of how fast I had moved in our work together after just one session.

When he left me on the front porch that afternoon,

I was in tears. He asked me to consider his methods, and if I agreed to live on the farm, he assured me I would become a different person. I still can't understand how he got me to admit the bit about my son. The picture in the cigar box was my infant son who had died a few days after he was born. He hadn't been given up for adoption. He hadn't been stolen. That was a story I had always told myself since I was a teenager. Hartley's ideas of storytelling weren't completely foreign to me. The only difference was that the delusion I'd lived with didn't take, and it certainly hadn't taken away the pain.

So I decided to trust Hartley. If for no other reason than to get clean and to pursue my search for Mom. I became increasingly convinced that she was at the farm, that I was close to her. When Hartley came back out on the porch for my decision, I jumped up out of my seat and threw my arms around him. I collapsed in his grip. It didn't bother me that he reeked of French fries and vinegar. He comforted me. Then he said that I had to remove the toxins from my body before we could go any further and that we had to start right away. He asked me if I had any contraband and, if so, to relinquish it to him immediately. I emptied my pockets of some junk and gave him the keys to Henrietta. Told him that all I had was in that car. This gesture of openness impressed him. I'm surprised I did it, looking back now. I'd been swept away by the power of his promises. I was also at the end of the line and didn't see any other options.

Hartley showed me upstairs and told me to take a bath and lie down. He left a large white robe for me hanging on the door. I didn't overthink any of it. I just followed what he directed me to do. I think I was just so goddamn blasted that I was ready to float away or disintegrate. I remember a brief moment in the tub when I submerged my head completely under and looked up at the ceiling through a sheath of water. I remember combing my hair with an antique comb with a wooden handle, and I remember thinking that the bed in the upstairs guest room was the most comfortable thing in the world. I don't remember waking up or how I wound up in the barn.

They called it the dormitory. It had been converted into a fully functioning domicile. There were two levels. On the main floor, beds in rows lined the perimeter. Upstairs were a kitchen and an open-concept living room. It must have cost a fortune to repurpose the place. It wasn't fancy, but it certainly functioned well. I stayed in that reconverted barn for three weeks—twenty-one days. I'm clearer on the details of the last seven or eight days than of those first two weeks.

I lived with Hartley's women. The ones I'd seen reading in the fields on that first afternoon. Close up, I was less freaked out by them. In fact, I took to them almost immediately, as they acted as my caregivers through those endless, gruesome hours of my detox. I was cared for by fifty of the most loving, caring, gentle souls I'd ever encountered. They took turns sitting by my bedside. They held cold cloths on my forehead. There was soup—endless bowls of the stuff. I'd fall asleep in the embrace of one of them and wake up in the arms of another. They were patient and calm. They withstood my fits and bouts of ranting. If I didn't sleep, they stayed up with me. Surely this is the only antidote for pain—the unrelenting, boundless love of a mother's touch. Imagine being cared for by a mass of mothers. I still saw them all as one. At first, it didn't matter which one was the real one, the one who'd given birth to me. They all treated me with the warmth that I'd been so desperate for all of my life.

The healing happened quickly in this way. I wanted to be better because they wanted me to be better. Because their caring was so very real and tangible, I began to care for myself. I shuddered at the idea of having ever harmed myself. The idea of relapsing never entered my brain. It would be such a betrayal of all their work.

The greatest part about my time with the mothers was when they'd read to me. Or that's what I remember most anyway. It was only then that I started to differentiate between them and start to see them as individuals. I heard all kinds of different stories. Magical stories. Not fairy tales but stories of adventure and freedom filled with humour and triumph—these were the stories of their lives.

Donna's was set in the middle of a circus. She was a trapeze artist who had been discovered by a Romanian master one day on her way to work. Donna was running late when she got stuck in traffic. Instead of remaining stuck, she jumped out of her car, climbed a hydro pole, and fearlessly began to walk above the streets on the live wire.

Elma was an inventor in hers. She created eyeglasses that could reveal the true nature of people when looking at them through the magical lenses. If a person were full of shit, the glass would turn purple. If a person were a liar, it would turn green. If they were honest and loving, the glass would glow blue. It meant that there were no assholes in her life.

There were other inventors too. Beth created a cup that she would fill with water, and it would pour out chocolate. Lucille had a remote control that she could point at anyone bitching and complaining in order to silence them. Some were less high-tech. Delores perfected perfume that made her smell like apple pie. She loved apple pie.

Norma told of the time when she sprinted the Appalachian Trail in just one night. She'd planned it for years, figuring out all of the best routes, learning how to speak fox, bear, moose, and deer. When the day came, she was able to do in twenty-four hours what takes most adventurers six months.

Gretchen had a habit of losing things every day: her keys, her wallet, her purse, her kids. But whatever she lost, within minutes of losing it, she'd find a replacement that always turned out to be much better than the original. This was how she'd been marrying a string of men, each one better than the last.

In Florence's story, men didn't exist. They'd all been misplaced. Lost and never found.

Wilma had a different approach. In her story, men did exist but only in tiny sizes—like the size of salt and pepper shakers. In fact, she kept her husband and two sons on top of the counter next to the paprika, her boss, her uncle Louis, and her father-in-law.

In Celeste's story, no one ever died. Ever. In all the history of the world, no one had ever perished. It wasn't allowed. She spent her days collecting autographs and getting her picture taken with the likes of Margaret Laurence, Joan of Arc, Cleopatra, Marilyn Monroe, and Clark Gable.

Those were the silly stories. But there were others as well, beautiful stories. The ones I liked best of all were the ones about the families of fish. The woman who told them was the woman whom I believed to be my mother, so I took to calling her Winifred. She never told me her real name, and I never asked. She was the oldest of them.

Winifred's stories were the most simple. In them, she was the keeper of a giant aquarium. This aquarium stretched out endlessly so that there was no start point and no end point in sight. This meant that no matter where you stood, you were always watching from the middle, surrounded by a glass wall like a window into the ocean. The woman was never a major character in her stories. In fact, she was usually absent from the plot.

Yet, she was always present in how she was the one who witnessed the unfolding of events inside the aquarium. Moreover, all the creatures that lived inside were described as her creatures. She recounted the adventures of all kinds of different species. I liked the ones about the sea horses. But most of all, I responded to the ones about the mouthbrooder fish that hold their offspring in their mouths for extended periods. Oral incubation. I was taken by these stories of the pikehead fish and the lumpfish that would hold their children in their mouths to keep them free from harm.

As the days passed and my mind became more lucid, they were the only stories that I cared to remember. The women read their stories to me from their notebooks. Doc Hartley was right; they were perfecting the practice. They kept their books with them wherever they went. Usually tucked inside a pocket or under their arms. They slept with the books under their pillows. Took them with them into the bathroom.

In that last week of my recovery, I began to become concerned for this practice. The stories made me laugh, dream, forget, but outside of what they read to me, we didn't really speak to one another. Besides pleasantries: "How are you?" "Nice day." "Roasted or mashed for supper?"

By the time I'd reached a real sense of clarity, I felt worried for these women. It's true that they didn't live in fear. That they were free from pain. That they lived in beautiful worlds where they were the heroes. But their state seemed too fragile. One day, Donna might actually try climbing a hydro pole and be electrocuted; Elma would have to encounter an asshole; Beth's cup would be filled with mud, not chocolate; Norma might get eaten by a bear; Gretchen might lose herself and not be able to find herself again; Florence and Wilma would meet men who were life-size; Celeste's cat, Garland, would die. What then? Maybe that's why I really only held onto Winifred's stories of the aquarium and the mouthbrooder lumpfish. They were lovely and vivid and weren't contingent on suspending the laws of the natural world. The woman who told them didn't fly carpets or cure diseases; she told her stories to remind herself of the mysterious wonders of the world. A world as an aquarium. An observation deck for life.

I can't be certain, but since I wanted that mother to be my mother, I accepted her as my mother. They all treated me the same loving way, and I responded accordingly, but I held the belief inside me that she was the one.

27

By the time the three weeks were up, I'd never felt stronger. I breathed differently. I moved differently. I'd gained ten pounds from good eating, so my ribs no longer jutted out. The most dramatic change was in relation to time. There were so many more hours in a day. I remember being in awe of simple things: the sky, the wind, my hands. When the women took to the fields that morning for their silent reading, I joined them and wandered around the property among them.

It was my first walk outside since getting clean. Autumn was in the air, and I embraced the chill and the colour of the brilliant leaves. By then, I was convinced that Winifred, the old aquarium keeper, was my mother. She had to be. Beneath a round, wrinkled face were two piercing aquamarine eyes that were exactly the colour and shape of my own. She was my height, although she was hunched, which made her appear shorter. We were the same build. She was dressed like the rest of them, so there wasn't much else to go on.

Learning what I had from Hartley, I knew she was

someone else now, and she couldn't possibly remember me. It was worse than that actually. An intrusion from me would compromise her stories, the ones she'd been telling herself and perfecting through the years. I knew I couldn't intrude for fear of where it would leave her. But I needed something, even a glance or a smile. If I could get that, I'd know that somewhere inside her she knew. Then I'd leave her be. I certainly wouldn't bring up Dad. There was no point. He'd have been long since turned into tilapia and eaten by a shark. But I needed some acknowledgement.

I found her sitting by a small pond. She was dutifully reading from her notebook. Breathlessly mouthing the words. I'd seen them doing this for weeks now and observed their trancelike state as something holy and not to be disturbed. There was a real energy between the notebook and the movements of her mouth. I wanted just to sidle up beside her, maybe put my arm around her gently. But I felt Hartley's hand on my shoulder instead. He led me back to the house.

As we walked, he told me he was pleased with my work—proud too. I told him that I felt fantastic, and I did, like a new woman. There was something demeaning in his face when I said this. According to him, I was getting ahead of myself. It was time to move onto phase two of the treatment. Where the real work would begin.

Before we entered the house, I noticed that Henrietta was no longer parked out front—sideways, straight ways, or any ways. The car was gone. Hartley said he'd taken care of it for me. He said it was important to relinquish anything and everything from the past. The money inside was gone too.

I suppose if I'd been in the place where I was before getting healthy, I'd have gone for his balls or kicked his teeth in, or maybe started screaming—something. But I didn't. I think I may have laughed when he told me the news. I knew if I started to question him and his methods, I'd probably end up where I started or find myself worse off than before. It was a big decision, following him into that house. One that I made in the time it took to get from the bottom of the front steps to inside the front hall. It would mean that I would have to see this thing through. I saw myself climbing the steps and walking inside. It was a bold move, and I made it. I sat down across from Hartley at his desk. He pulled out a file folder.

"Before we go any further," he said, "I have something here that you may want to see. I should tell you that if I show it to you, it may make the work you have to do that much more difficult. If you're going to set out to rewrite the past, it may be easier for you if you don't know the particulars of certain details."

"What is it?"

"This is Winifred McKeagan's file. I dug it out from my records."

I regarded the thing with severity. It was just a stack of papers, but it was evidence—the proof I thought I was after.

"Shall I show it to you? It may be a real setback."
"How so?"

"You have a picture of her in your head. You painted it. It's based on your memories. However distorted or fractured, it exists and it's yours. Then you have your desires. Again, they're all your own. They belong to you. These are what you want to be true. I take it that what you remember and what you want to be true may be at odds. That's easy to correct. You begin to doubt and reinvent until a new picture comes into focus. This folder would upset both your memory and your desires. It may throw you into a kind of chaos. And then what? It will take a lot more work after that, regardless of what you find hiding in here."

He placed the folder on his desk and folded his hands together, placing them on top. He had a valid point. More than that, I was afraid to look. I remember her in pain. I remember her depressed and high. I remember her bruised. I remember her in constant battle with Dad. But I also remember glimpses of warmth: a stroll in the park, bath time, kisses. Or maybe I don't. Maybe these were my desires. I wanted her to be the old woman in the fields, telling stories about the mouthbrooder fish. I wanted her to be safe. I wanted her to be free of pain. I wanted her to remember me. But if it turned out that it wasn't her out there by the pond, then what? The folder could reveal something even worse: that she was dead. To come so close to her, to feel her hands on my forehead and hear her voice telling me stories, only to have her vanish, evaporate into thin air in an instant. It was too risky.

"I don't want to see it," I said.

"Very good." Hartley stood up and moved to the fireplace. He dug in his pockets and produced a lighter. He set the papers on fire and tossed them inside. I watched the bright orange embers burn to black. Then he returned to his desk and sat down.

"I'm proud of your decision," he said, "and you should be proud too."

I didn't feel proud. I felt like a coward. I felt afraid.

Hartley brought me upstairs next and sat me down in a high-back chair in front of a large mirror. I already had blunt bangs, but he took out a pair of sharp scissors and, in one cut, chopped off my long braid. It fell to the floor. Then he wet and combed the rest back and made it like the others'. He looked at me in the mirror, trimmed some more, and then left me to change into a polka dot dress.

I'd become one of Hartley's women.

He was waiting for me downstairs. "I have something else for you. It's something you will need to keep with you from now on and at all times." He held out a package wrapped in teal tissue paper.

"A gift?" I asked.

"No, my dear, the real gift is what you do with it." He handed it to me, beaming.

I opened it up. It was a notebook, leather-bound and red. I flipped through the crisp pages. It was a beautiful book. It fit perfectly in my hands.

"Take it at your own pace," he said. "It won't come all at once. You need to be patient and practice. And when you're ready to begin your story, you will know."

I knew I was taking part in some kind of rehearsed ritual that had been played out before. I'd been introduced to the results of the practice in the barn already. That was surely Hartley's method. He knew that I loved those women, that I had nothing but respect for them. I suppose he thought that the notion of a notebook of my very own would be all the convincing I'd need. Truth be told, I was very happy to have it. I held the book close to me, and with my new dress and hairdo, I crossed the field and went back to my little spot inside the barn.

28

At first, nothing came. I had writer's block. I had only just begun to plan out my story, but all roads were leading me back to real places. I pictured myself being born into a family of musicians who played in a band. The father played guitar, the mother sang, and the kids played rhythm and horns. It seemed like a good start, but it reminded me of the time when my father hawked my brother's drum kit at the pawnshop downtown to pay for a gambling debt. So that didn't work out too well.

I tried a new approach next; I went more exotic. I'd been born in the jungle. My parents were anthropologists looking for a new species of bird when my mother became pregnant with me. I'd grown up living in a tree house, eating berries and leaves. Then I remembered Scuzzy and Boner. They entered the picture, and that tale was shot to hell.

It seemed that no matter where I began, it was nothing more than a shit fantasy that couldn't compete with the real past. In one version, I was rich, a princess. I laughed my ass off at the thought of my father as king of anything. Court jester maybe. In another version, I'd be poor. But seeing as how we really were poor, it wasn't long before I was stealing lipstick from the drugstore to pay for dope. Real life continuously intruded and took me out of my stories. Of course, it didn't help that I didn't have a pen. Hartley had said I'd get one when I was ready to commit. I was ready to give up.

Then I had a breakthrough. I had been trying to invent the past, as opposed to reinventing it. That is, I had been basing everything on pure make-believe, and so it was next to impossible to believe it. If I were to start with some truths and then reinvent the rest, I thought that maybe the creative juices would start to flow. And they did, at first.

I began with what I knew: I was born into a working-class family in Oshawa, Ontario. I had five brothers, a mother, and a father. I focused on major events, things that may have set our lives in a certain direction. The death of my little brother, Pete, for example. It had destroyed my mother. In my new story, Pete didn't die. In my story, Pete was a kind of miracle child who was given an opportunity to remain a child forever and go on playing games in various playgrounds around the world. It was sad to say goodbye to the boy, but if it meant he would have a fabulous life, then so be it.

Then I focused on other events. Liam got busted for arson and thrown out of school? Not true! He graduated with honours two years early. My father threw a bottle of red wine against the wall when the Leafs lost in overtime?

Nope! It was a pie at a pie-throwing contest, and Dad won—and so did the Leafs, incidentally. My mother hadn't tried to kill herself. She was practicing ballroom dancing down in the basement. She was so good, in fact, that we all drove her to her dance recital in Saint John, New Brunswick. After that, we drove around in a limo because we were a celebrity family. So well-liked that I didn't have to go to school after grade nine or ever get a job. Instead, I met a real poet named Trevor, who introduced me to rhyming couplets, not LSD, and we had a child who was so beautiful and healthy and who didn't suffer from fetal alcohol syndrome and who came out of me speaking fourteen different languages and was able to sing too, and we knew the world needed him and that we couldn't keep him all to ourselves, so we showcased him at travelling museums and fairs and amusement parks to bring hope to everyone who saw him. I never fought with Dad. Instead, we started a boxing club together for recovering alcoholics. Uncle Dirk was a ventriloquist who played the vaudeville circuit—a star of silent films, the last vaudevillian. Ma Edna's house was made of cookies and cake.

And on and on like this. I was picking apart every hurt, every piece of dysfunction, delinquency, and trash, and reinventing a magical past for myself. I think it was working too. I started to dream these dreams night and day. There wasn't much else to do on the farm. I didn't have to worry about food or money. The only thing that kept me from completely moving into my reinvented world was the issue of the man I called Tongue.

He appeared one day during an outing some of us took with Hartley. If he hadn't, if I had been able to erase him from my mind, or if I simply never remembered him at all, things may have worked out differently.

Some time had passed. I'm not sure how long, but it's safe to say that I'd given up doubting Hartley, and I was anxious to start writing down my story in words. Hartley still refused to give me a pen though. He said that the more I thought about the story, the richer it would become.

At first, I hadn't been permitted to go along on errands, but as Hartley saw my continued commitment to the work, he invited me to join him and three or four of the women for a bit of grocery shopping in Summerside. It was somebody's birthday (I can't remember whose), and we always had wonderful dinners when it was somebody's birthday. The list was divided up between us, and we went off to pick up what we'd been assigned. Hartley had given us forty dollars each.

I wasn't even supposed to buy the fish. It was on Gwendolyn's list, but she had asked to trade with me because she hated the smell of fish. I agreed even though I was looking forward to picking out the ice cream. The sign in the market for the fish counter directed customers outside to the pier. Apparently, a fresh shipment had come in, and you could go buy fish directly from the fisherman. I wandered out of the store and walked down to the harbour.

I saw the boat first before reading its name painted in gold letters: *The More or Less*. Then I saw him: Tongue, on board separating shellfish into buckets. He wore a giant navy-blue peacoat with a huge white scarf wrapped around his neck. He had on enormous gloves with the fingers cut out. On his head sat my father's chauffeur's hat, which looked more like a sea captain's cap now, pierced through with a tiny gold hook.

There was no sign of Morella or Lester.

I approached cautiously. Panicked. Confused. My brain hurt. When I made it to the edge of the dock, a large, black, shaggy dog—a beautiful Newfoundlander—bounded over to me and jumped up on me, its paws on my shoulders. The dog licked my face with a massive, hot, wet tongue. The force from the animal nearly knocked me to the ground.

Tongue looked up from his work on the boat and called out to the dog: "Brody! Heeere!"

Or maybe it was "Rosie." I can't be sure. Either way, the beast got off me and raced towards the water, leapt about ten feet in the air, and landed in the boat. Tongue and Brody looked over the edge of the boat and stared at me while their two long pink tongues dangled down. I was frozen in place on that boardwalk. Since abandoning Tongue back in Saint John months earlier, I'd not thought about him once. I'm not sure how I'd been able to do this, or what kind of sick act of survival it was, but I had removed him from my mind.

"I blot da bloat! I blot da bloat!"

Hartley whisked me away. Or that's how I'll choose to remember it happening. I may have run off myself. Maybe I wasn't forced at all. But I got out of there in a hurry without saying a word to the man on the boat. By the time we got back to the farm, however, the damage of that encounter had been done. I could no longer concentrate on rewriting my past. This was because I'd encountered the one thing in my life that didn't deserve to be rewritten. More than that, it was the one thing in my life that was larger, more magical, and more beautiful than anything I could ever invent. That episode marked my decline on the farm. From that moment on, I became distrustful. The next morning, I went to see Hartley.

"How's the story coming along?"

"I'm stuck."

"Oh?"

"I remembered someone who I can't forget. He can't be erased."

"You're not supposed to erase. You are to reshape."

"He can't be reshaped either. He's too big. Too extraordinary."

"Who is he?"

"I call him Tongue. He rescued me from home."

"You've never mentioned him before."

"I thought he'd disappeared on his own. It was painful leaving him the way I did. I didn't want to. He was the only person who'd ever been kind to me."

"I see. When did you meet him?"

"On the day my father died."

"Really? Well that's convenient. And what did you two do together?"

"We travelled here together in the limo."

"Limo, eh? Why do you call him Tongue?"

"Because he has a big tongue. It's huge. It sticks out of his mouth like a big fish. He's like an overgrown child. I can't rewrite him. He's perfect the way he is."

"Sounds a bit farfetched. Almost mythical. Maybe you should keep him in the story then. Write him in."

Hartley thought I was making him up. It was impossible to leave him out of my story, and it would be impossible to leave him in and remain on the farm. Tongue had enabled me to escape. I saw that now. To acknowledge his presence was to acknowledge his role in my life. And to do that, I'd need to remember what had happened. The real sequence of things. Of course, I didn't tell Hartley this. I just agreed with him.

"Keep plotting it out," he said. "If it's important to keep this so-called Tongue, then by all means you should keep him."

When I got back to the barn, the mothers were celebrating yet another birthday party. With fifty women inventing so many lives, we had birthday parties nearly every night. It was a lovely time though. The fish and potato dinner was delicious. I was happy to spend time with a group of such strong, spirited women. I never once judged them for living within their make-believe worlds. In my own way, I was inspired by Hartley's work.

I stayed up that night thinking about how to start the story in light of Tongue's intrusion. I soon realized that it had to begin with the moment I met Tongue. I would have to start there. It wasn't the fact that Dad died that made that day important; it was because it was the day I met Tongue. The direction had never been so clear in my head.

I was restless thinking about it. I couldn't sleep. I got up to make myself some warm milk. It was extremely late, maybe three or four in the morning. I thought everyone was asleep. Winifred slept at the far end of the barn. I noticed that her light was on. I went over to her. She looked to be trying to read from her book but kept nodding off. She was lying down, and she held the book in front of her, resting it on her chest. Each time she began to doze, the book would slip and hit her in the face. It would wake her up, and she'd open her eyes, slightly startled. I observed this for a few moments, maybe longer. Then she noticed me standing there by her bed.

"Hi, dear. I seem to be falling asleep," she said.

I went over to her then and sat down beside her on the bed.

"How's your story coming?" she asked me.

"I think I may have a good idea," I said. "I've been struggling to begin, but I think I know where I want to go."

"Wonderful, dear. Write one about the ocean. It's so endless and beautiful."

"I just may do that," I said.

She was falling deeper under, really struggling to stay awake. "That's wonderful, dear." As she said this, she dropped the book against her face, and it slipped off and landed on the floor.

I got up quietly so as not to disturb her and pulled the covers up to her chin. Then I reached down to retrieve the book. Before placing it under her pillow, I flipped open a few pages. They were blank. I turned more pages. These were blank also. The whiteness of the paper stared back at me. I closed the book and placed it under her head. Then I bent down and kissed the woman on the forehead and turned out her light.

Just to confirm my suspicion, I went around the barn that night and stole glimpses of as many of their books as I could. Ingrid's was blank; Norma's was blank; Donna's: blank; Rachael's, Irene's, Mildred's—all of them—all blank. Not one word had been written in any of the books.

I made it back to my bunk, out of breath. My adrenalin was pumping. I opened up my red leather notebook that Doc Hartley had given to me as the answer to my suffering. It was just as blank as the rest of them. I swore on that night that I would not leave it that way. It meant that I had to leave.

So just before dawn on that cold late-November morning, clad in my polka dot dress, sporting a blunt A-line bob with baby bangs, my blank notebook under my arm, I walked out of that barn and out of Doc Hartley's potato farm in North Rustico, Prince Edward Island.

The red dirt road before me was pitch-black. I was on foot. There was no moon, but I wasn't afraid. I knew where I was in relation to the water, and I could even hear the tide as I got closer to the shore. Then a vehicle crept up the path behind me. It was the battered and bruised Henrietta. The limo pulled over to the side of the road, and the window was lowered. Shep's sleep-smashed face popped out.

"Where ya off to?" he asked me.

"I'm gonna take a walk."

"A bit late out, don't you think? Or maybe a bit early?"

"I'm not going back to the farm."

"No," he said, "I can't imagine that you would. But she's bloody cold out. I'll drive ya wherever you're going."

"Take me to the harbour," I said.

Shep rolled up the window, and I got inside the back of the long limousine.

"You going to see the big fella, ain't ya? You know, he bought *The More or Les*. Been doing pretty darn good for himself too. When he's not catching, he's ferrying folks between Scotia, Brunny, and the Island. Even headed out to Labrador once or twice according to my cousin Les."

"Did they ever make it to Egypt?"

"Nope. But after selling the boat, they moved to Toronto."

"Bad idea."

"That's what I says."

When we got to the harbour, the sun was just about to rise. A group of fishermen huddled together and discussed the weather and their wives. Steam from their coffee cups rose into the misty air. I opened the door and climbed out.

"Keep the car," I told Shep.

"Thanks."

I could see that Shep didn't want to just leave me there, but I told him to.

"Don't even want to wait in the limo?" he asked me.

I didn't, and as he drove away, I knew I'd never have to see the car again.

There was a reluctant, sluggish flow of activity as the fishermen loaded their boats, unfastened ropes, and began their preparations for the day's work on the water. Still, I could hear them laughing and telling jokes. Then I heard a foghorn blast that lit up and rattled the harbour. The horn was followed by the familiar sound of a certain singer. This was accompanied by the yelps and yips of a dog.

Tongue docked *The More or Les* and tied her to the pier. Brody bounded toward me and licked my hands.

"I'm looking for lumpfish," I said. "The kind that keep the baby fish in their mouths."

"Get on," Tongue said to me.

I climbed aboard the fishing boat and took my place beside the singing sailor.

"It's bloody freezing out," I said. "Christ almighty! Do you have any coffee?"

Tongue disappeared down below and returned with a Thermos the size of a trumpet case. Then he untied the boat and began to steer clear of the other vessels.

I unscrewed the lid. The contents of the cylinder were creamy white and smelled like rancid spew. "Yuck! What the hell do you have in here?"

"Chowder."

"Stinks."

"Got dome doughnuts too," Tongue said as he jammed a bear claw into his trap.

I patted Brody vigorously. "Nice. I'm gonna need a pen too. I'm writing a book."

"Nice. 'Bout what?"

"Your tongue," I told him.

When I said this, Tongue started to laugh. Then he stuck the thing out at me like a child as he gunned *The More or Less* and we pulled out towards the mouth of the ocean.